PURRFECT BOY TOY

THE MYSTERIES OF MAX 18

NIC SAINT

PURRFECT BOY TOY

The Mysteries of Max 18

Edited by Chereese Graves

www.nicsaint.com

Give feedback on the book at: info@nicsaint.com

facebook.com/nicsaintauthor
@nicsaintauthor

First Edition

Printed in the U.S.A

1

"But I don't *want* to go to LA!"

"You're going, whether you like it or not," said Gran, giving me a hard look. "And so am I."

"Um, I never said anything about you going to LA, Gran," said Odelia.

"Of course I'm going," Gran snapped. "You don't think I'm going to let my favorite grandchild go off to that hellhole on her own, do you?"

"I'm your only grandchild, and I hardly think LA is a hellhole."

Gran wagged a finger in her granddaughter's face. "Everybody knows LA is one of the most dangerous places on the planet, full of gangs and movie stars and whatnot. And I'm not going to stand idly by while you land yourself in a steaming heap of trouble, missy."

I would have pointed out that movie stars are not all that dangerous, but I had a feeling my words would fall on deaf ears. When Gran gets something in her noggin it's hard to get it out. She definitely hadn't listened when I told her in no uncertain terms I didn't want to go on this impromptu trip, and neither did Dooley. Not that we don't enjoy the occasional holiday, but we don't like flying. The whole prospect of being cooped up inside an iron tube that hovers a couple of miles above the earth's surface has never filled me with particular joy, and it certainly didn't do so now.

"Gran, the invitation didn't mention a plus-one, so I'm afraid—"

"Well, I'm not leaving you to fight this battle on your own, Odelia. Not on my watch."

We were in Odelia's living room, which, coincidentally, is also my living room, and Gran was standing her ground, even though technically this was Odelia's ground. But then Gran considers any turf her own turf, so there's that to consider.

"I'll have to ask," said Odelia dubiously, and took out her phone.

"Do that, and while you're at it, double check if pets are allowed."

Odelia nodded and held the phone to her ear.

I turned to Dooley, who had been following the negotiation with trepidation.

"I don't want to go to LA, Max," he said. "We have cat choir and my solo is coming up."

"So is mine," I said, "and I'm sure Odelia will realize that singing our solo is much more important than flying off to some godforsaken place called Los Angeles."

"Can't Chase go with her? I'm sure he's much better equipped to deal with this case than we are. We don't even know our way around this LA place."

"Another very good argument," I said, nodding, and I ticked them off on my claws. "First off, flying is not safe. Planes fall from the sky every day. Everybody knows this. Second, Gran is there to help her out. And third, Chase should go, as he's a cop, and cops are better equipped to deal with troubled celebrity talk show hosts than cats are."

"And don't forget about my solo," said Dooley.

"Of course. How could I forget?" I said with a smile.

Recently cat choir had instigated a new rule about solo performances. Used to be that Harriet, our Persian cat friend, was the only one allowed to sing solos, but several of cat choir's members didn't think that this was fair. And so Shanille, cat choir's director, decided that she was done excluding cats from stepping into the limelight. In one of those groundbreaking decisions she declared that everyone should be allowed to sing a solo. And since tonight was finally Dooley's turn, it was obvious we couldn't leave for Los Angeles on a moment's notice. He'd simply forfeit his turn and then who knew how long it would be before he got to go again. And he'd been practicing so hard, too.

"You have to tell her, Max," he repeated now, a testament to his anguish.

"You can tell her, too," I said. "She'll listen to you."

"Yes, but you're her favorite, Max."

"No, I'm not."

"Yes, you are. You're her first, and no one ever forgets their first."

"Um… pretty sure you're referring to something else entirely," I said.

"Harriet says so, too. She says you're Odelia's favorite and she always does whatever you tell her to. So please, please, please, Max, don't make her take me to this LA place!"

"Okay, okay, okay," I said, holding up my paws. Then: "Harriet told you that?"

"She did."

"So… she's talking to you?"

"Of course. Why wouldn't she?"

Well, she wasn't talking to me, that was for sure. Ever

since I voted in favor of Shanille's new soloist rule, she'd refused to utter a single word to me. Which wasn't fair, since Brutus and Dooley had voted for the new rule, too. Brutus had done so when Harriet wasn't looking, of course, the sneaky cat, and Dooley had simply sneezed and Shanille had taken that as a yes, something Harriet could hardly hold against him.

"Do you think Harriet and Brutus will be there tonight?" asked Dooley, relaxing now that he knew I had his case well in hand, and the Los Angeles menace had been averted.

"I don't think so, Dooley. Harriet is still very cross about the whole soloist thing."

"She shouldn't be. We all should get the chance to shine," he said, repeating Shanille's words. "Everyone can sing, Max, even me."

I had a feeling Shanille had seen the movie *Sing* one too many times, but had refrained from voicing this thought. Shanille had once kicked me out of cat choir and I wasn't going to risk her ire over a trifling matter like who got to sing the solos.

"I know, Dooley, but she took it really hard."

"Maybe she can go tomorrow?" he suggested.

"Tomorrow is my solo," I pointed out.

"Yes, but you could let her take your place. She'd love that."

I stared at him. "Take my place? But it's my turn to shine, Dooley."

"I know, but Harriet has been so sad lately. And you know you can't really sing, Max."

This was true. I'm probably cat choir's worst singer. Still, if everyone can sing, I can sing, too. At least if Shanille was to be believed. Besides, Harriet had been more angry than sad. As far as I can tell Harriet doesn't do sad. It hadn't been fun for the rest of us. As I pointed out before, Harriet is a

Persian, and when Persians get angry they don't stint on the anger. I think she even peed in my water bowl. I mean, I couldn't prove it, of course, but lately my water had had a distinctly weird taste and odor. Not fresh, I mean.

"Why don't you give her your spot?" I said.

"But Max! I've been waiting for so long—and I've practiced so hard. I can't let her take my spot. Besides, I can't disappoint my fans—they're all waiting to hear me sing."

I rolled my eyes. Everyone can sing. And apparently everyone is a diva, too.

Meanwhile, Odelia had returned, Gran in tow. She was still talking into her phone, apparently trying to get her grandmother added to the guest list.

"Tell her I'm her biggest fan," Gran was saying, and Odelia gestured for her to be quiet.

"I feel bad about this, Max," Dooley intimated. "We've never turned down a case before."

"I know. I feel bad about it, too."

It had all begun last night. We'd been ready to go to bed, Odelia upstairs brushing her teeth and Chase reading in bed, when Odelia's phone had belted out its merry tune.

"Can you get that?!" Odelia shouted from the bathroom, her mouth full of toothpaste.

Chase had grabbed her phone from the nightstand and picked up.

It had been none other than Opal Harvey herself, the queen of daytime talk shows. She'd gotten Odelia's information from her dear friend Marilyn Coyn, a talk show host in her own right, and Opal's BFF, and told Chase she had a case for Odelia to take on.

By the time Odelia had hurriedly spat out her toothpaste and talked to the famous woman, her eyes were shining with anticipation, and even Chase sat up a little straighter.

It isn't every day that celebrity royalty rings you up and

tells you they need you and can you please drop everything and fly out to LA, all expenses paid, to take on a case.

Odelia had sputtered for a while, claiming she wasn't qualified, that she was just a local reporter and not some famous detective, but Opal Harvey can be very convincing, and if that hadn't sealed the deal, the paycheck she'd dangled in front of Odelia like a carrot to a donkey had certainly helped. The moment Opal got off the phone Odelia was jumping up and down, chanting, "We're going to LA! We're going to meet Opal Harvey!"

Chase had grinned like a little boy, as starstruck as Odelia. And I have to confess I wasn't averse to meeting the famous woman myself, if only she hadn't lived on the other coast, and meeting her involved stepping onto a plane. We'd flown to England not that long ago to meet real royalty, and even though the plane hadn't crashed, that didn't mean it couldn't happen the next time. You have to respect the odds and I wasn't taking any chances. We'd survived a plane ride once, I wasn't willing to tempt fate by going again.

As luck would have it, though, Chase was flying to LA himself, and even though he was booked on a separate flight, and probably not first class, my mind was at ease: Chase would be there to assist Odelia, and from the looks of things, so would Grandma Muffin.

"And? What did she say?" asked Gran eagerly. As a big fan of daytime television—her love for soap operas is legendary—she was dying to meet the one and only Opal.

Odelia smiled. "Opal says it's okay. You can come."

"Yippie!" said Gran, and did a little jig in place. "I knew she'd agree!"

"Great," I said. "That means we don't have to go."

"Oh, you're going," said Odelia.

"But, Odelia!"

"You're going," she said, "and you're going," she told

Dooley, "and you're going," she said as Harriet walked in through the pet flap, "and you're going," she finished when Brutus entered on his mate's heels.

"Going where?" asked Harriet.

"We're going to LA, baby!" Gran cried.

2

"Did you really have to take all of them?" Gran grumbled.

Odelia smiled. "It was your idea to bring all four of them along, remember?"

"I'm not talking about the cats. I'm talking about those losers over there," said Gran, jerking her thumb in the direction of the rest of the company.

When Odelia talked to Opal on the phone, the talk show host had assured her she could bring whomever she wanted. She was sending her private jet to pick them up, and since it could hold at least a dozen, she could bring along any pets, grannies or other next of kin. As long as she made her way to LA pronto, since there was no time to waste.

Gran glared at Marge and Tex as they gave her a jolly little wave.

"I don't get why they had to tag along," she said, still grumbling. "What about Tex's patients. What are they going to say?"

"The same could be said about you, Gran. You work at the doctor's office, too."

"They won't miss me, but they sure as heck are going to miss Tex."

Tex had called in his good friend Cary Horsfield, who worked as a doctor in Hampton Keys, and was his bandmate in The Singing Doctors, to take over for him while he engaged in this little trip out west.

"And what about Marge? She can't just close up the library like that. People need their books. Reading is important."

"The library isn't closed, Gran. Marcie is taking over for a couple of days."

Marcie Trapper was Marge's neighbor, and didn't mind helping out her friend.

"It's not right," Gran muttered. "Opal invited *us*, not them." She directed an icy glare at Chase and Uncle Alec, who'd unanimously decided to ditch their official cattle class ride and hitch a ride on Opal's multi-million-dollar jet. It was a no-brainer, as they could travel in luxury, accompanied by their nearest and dearest—though Gran obviously didn't feel the same way about her son and Odelia's boyfriend joining them.

"How about you?" asked Odelia. "You brought a plus-one."

Next to Gran, a handsome young man sat, staring out the window and sipping from a milk carton. He was dressed in skinny jeans and a tight T-shirt that accentuated his ripped physique. His blond hair was ruffled and blue eyes dreamy.

"You haven't even introduced us yet," Odelia added. She reached across her grandmother and thrust out her hand. "Hi, my name is Odelia. I'm Vesta's granddaughter."

"Oh, hi," said the young man, then shook Odelia's hand and gave her a confused smile. "Did you say you're Vesta's... granddaughter?"

"That's right. And that's my mom and dad over there. And

that man over there is Vesta's son Alec—my uncle. And the guy next to him is Chase Kingsley. My boyfriend."

"Oh, um..." He directed a hesitant look at Gran. "I thought you said you had no family, Vesta? That you were too young and wild to settle down?"

"You must have misheard," she snapped. "I had my kids young. Very, very young."

Which wasn't necessarily true, but Odelia decided not to rock the boat.

"Okay," said the young man, and put a straw to his lips to resume sucking from his milk carton.

"So... what's your name?" Odelia insisted. She was both curious and unrelenting. It was the reporter in her, used to asking tough questions and not taking no for an answer.

"Oh, I'm sorry," he said. "My name is Hank. Hank Peterson."

"Well, nice to meet you, Hank," she said, plastering an engaging smile on her face.

"Likewise," said Hank, and returned once more to sucking on his straw.

For a moment, Odelia managed to stay silent, then she whispered, "Who is he?"

Gran didn't bat an eye when she whispered back, "He's my boyfriend."

Odelia stared at her grandmother, then to Hank, and back to Gran. "Wait, what?"

"He's handsome, isn't he? Probably the handsomest boyfriend I've ever had."

"But..."

"But what? Aren't you happy for me?"

"Um... he's very young, isn't he?"

"He sure is," said Gran, directing a loving glance at her boyfriend.

"So... how did the two of you meet?"

"Oh, enough about Hank already. What are we going to do about them?"

"What do you mean?"

"Them!" she said, gesturing once again to Tex and Marge, who were clearly enjoying their first flight on a private jet. "We need to ditch them! Get rid of the dead weight."

"We can't ditch them, Gran. They're family. You don't ditch family."

"What is Opal going to say when we show up with this sorry lot? She hired us, remember—two pros. Not June and Ward Cleaver."

In spite of herself, Odelia had to laugh. "I'm sure Opal will be fine."

"Fine! She hired two detectives and we're bringing her half a dozen!"

In all fairness Opal had only hired Odelia, with Gran attaching herself forcibly.

"What about Hank?" asked Odelia. "Is he a detective, too?"

"Oh, don't you mind Hank," said Gran with a wave of the hand. "He's with me."

Odelia grinned and settled back in her seat. She glanced over to her mother, who gave her two thumbs up and said, "Can't wait to meet her! Yay, Opal!"

"Yeah, yay, Opal," Gran muttered, clearly not happy with the state of affairs.

"I'm going to check on Max and the others," said Odelia, and got up. Moving to the back of the plane, she quickly found her feline brood. They were clearly having the time of their lives. When Odelia had told Opal she was bringing her cats along, the talk show host had been over the moon. An avid cat lover herself, she'd immediately given instructions for the airplane crew to give of their best when dealing with Max, Dooley, Harriet and Brutus, and now the foursome sat in their plush beige leather seats, snacking on what looked like some excellent gourmet food.

"So how are you guys doing?" she asked, settling in one of the sumptuous seats.

"Not too shabby," said Max as he tucked into what looked like prime paté covered in a gelatinous sauce.

"Who is the guy next to Gran?" asked Harriet.

Odelia glanced over her shoulder. "His name is Hank Peterson," she said, "and that's all I know." She lowered her voice. "Between you and me I think he's Gran's boy toy."

"Boy toy?" asked Dooley. "What's a boy toy?"

"It's when an older woman takes a younger man as her lover," said Harriet. "And frankly I think the term is insulting. When an older man takes a younger woman as his lover do they call her his girl toy? Well, do they?"

Odelia laughed. "No, I guess they don't."

"Boy toy," said Dooley, musing. "You mean he's not a real person but a toy?"

"No, he's a real person," Odelia said with a smile.

"He looks like a toy," said Harriet. "He looks like a Ken doll."

"Well, I can assure you he's real." She petted Dooley on the head and got up. "We'll be there soon, you guys, so eat up and enjoy your in-flight entertainment." She gestured to the big flatscreen in the corner, where a Garfield movie was playing.

"Boy toy," she heard Dooley say as she walked away. "Why not toy boy?"

"Oh, Dooley," said Harriet.

3

I had to admit that so far I was enjoying the experience. Last time we flew—also our first time—we'd been relegated to cages in the preliminary stages of the flight, and the experience hadn't been one I cared to remember. This time, however, limos had picked us up at the house, and had carried us straight to the airport, where this sleek little bird had been awaiting us, its flanks adorned with the letters OPAL AIR, indicating that this plane, evidently, belonged to Opal. No cages had been involved, and we'd simply walked aboard like normal cats, quickly to find ourselves engulfed in luxury and class.

"I think I like this, Max," said Dooley now, indicating he was on the same page.

"Yeah, I could get used to this," Brutus said with a satisfied grunt as he settled back and rubbed his belly contentedly. "In fact I only have one gripe."

"What's that?" I asked, wondering what there could be to cavil at on this super plane.

"That I don't have a bigger stomach," he said, and laughed uproariously.

"Ha ha," I said, though I thought the joke was a little crass. After all, the only reason we were on this flight was because our host and benefactor was suffering from some untold ordeal, and it would be rude of us to treat this as something other than what it was: a rescue mission. In fact it wasn't too much to say we were Opal's personal SEAL Team Six. Though CAT Team Four was perhaps the better description.

"I still think it's unfair that you would vote to end my career as a soloist," said Harriet suddenly, in fact the first time she'd spoken to me in three days.

"Well, you couldn't expect me to vote against the majority, Harriet," I pointed out.

"I could and you should have," she said, her eyes shooting a mild sheet of flame in my direction. "I'm your friend, Max. If I can't count on my friends, on who can I count?"

"On whom."

"Who cares! You should have told Shanille in no uncertain terms what you thought of her dictatorial ideas. And where she could stick them."

"That wouldn't have changed anything. She was going ahead with her soloist democratization plans regardless of what I or Dooley or anyone else thought about them. Besides, she got a clear majority, and cat choir is still a democracy last time I looked."

"No, it's not. It's a dictatorship and Shanille is its ruthless ruler."

There was no arguing with the cat, so I decided not to even try.

"If you want you can have my solo, Harriet," said Dooley now.

"Dooley," I said, looking up. "But I thought..."

"I was really looking forward to it, that's true," my friend said, "but I can see how much this means to Harriet, and since she's my friend I think she should have my spot."

"No, I couldn't possibly take your spot, Dooley," said Harriet.

"You know what?" I said. "You can have my spot, too."

"Max? Are you serious?" she said, her eyes wide.

"Sure. What else are friends for?"

"Oh, you guys," she said, her eyes brimming with unshed tears of gratitude. "I don't know what to say."

"Thank you would be nice," I said with a smile.

And then she flew down from her seat and hopped up onto Dooley's seat to give him a hug, repeating the procedure with me and giving me a big wet kiss on my nose to boot.

"Thanks," she said huskily. "I'll never forget this."

"You can have my spot, too," said Brutus.

"Oh, Brutus," she said.

"But I thought you quit cat choir?" said Dooley.

"Yeah, I did. But I can join up again, and then Harriet can take my spot."

Harriet was beaming. "This is the best day of my life!" she said, and then promptly dug into her paté with renewed fervor.

I frankly hoped we'd make it back to Hampton Cove in one piece, or else Harriet's star turn as cat choir's leading lady would never even materialize, in spite of our efforts to guarantee her a prime spot on its soloist roster. Even though the plane was top-notch, and so was the food and the accommodations, it still didn't make me lose sight of the fact that we were in a narrow steel tube, hurtling through space miles above the earth, and held up by forces I couldn't even begin to understand. Then again, if we did crash on a deserted island, we wouldn't be alone. My entire family was there with me, and we could simply start afresh wherever we landed. Gran, for one, seemed ready and willing to repopulate the earth, judging from the way she was intently staring at her boy toy. Or was it toy boy? Whatever he was, she was clearly enjoying the ride.

Four hours later, I was awoken by a gentle stirring of my shoulder, and when I opened my eyes I found myself gazing up into Odelia's lovely green peepers.

"We're almost there, you guys. Better get ready." And to show us what she meant by getting ready, she proceeded to strap us in with the little harnesses that had been provided especially for smallish passengers like ourselves.

"Do you think this is the plane Opal herself takes when she goes somewhere?" asked Harriet, whose mood had gone up a notch or two—or a dozen—since we departed.

"Yeah, this is Opal's private plane," said Odelia. "This is the one she takes all the time."

"So these seats..." said Harriet, patting the nice leather. "They're the same seats her own cat sits in?" Her voice had taken on a reverent tone.

Opal's cat is called Prunella, and is famous for accompanying her owner everywhere.

"Prunella must be really old by now," said Brutus. "I remember seeing that cat on TV when I was still living with Chase's mom."

"Yeah, Prunella is an old gal by now," said Odelia, and finished strapping Brutus in. "So when you meet her, you better be on your best behavior, you hear?"

"We're always on our best behavior," I said.

"First impressions are everything, you guys," said Harriet, "so Odelia is right. When we meet Prunella, be polite and act like gentlecats."

Next to me, Dooley was gritting his teeth, his claws digging into the armrests of his seat. "I hope we don't crash," he said. "This is the tricky part, isn't it? The landing."

"It'll be fine," I assured him. "We're not going to crash.

These pilots have brought us this far, and I'm sure they'll land this bird nice and easy."

He nodded, looking strained. "But what if we lose a wheel, Max? It happens. Or an engine? These wheels and engines have a habit of falling off for no good reason at all."

"Nothing is going to fall off. No wheels and no engines. Just stay calm and this will all be over with before you know it."

For some reason Brutus was grinning at me. "What?" I said. "What's so funny?"

"You," he said. "You look like a sausage in that harness. All strapped in like that."

I gave him my best supercilious look. Brutus is a dear friend, but he has a tendency to be crass. "I'll have you know that I am not a sausage," I said.

"Oh, don't be so touchy, Max," said Harriet. "It's a big advantage, you know."

"What is?"

"Being fat! All those layers of blubber will protect you if the plane goes down."

"Max?" said Dooley. "I don't like all this talk about planes going down."

"First of all, I'm not fat—I'm big-boned. And secondly, this plane isn't going down. We're perfectly safe."

"I wish I had those layers of lard," said Brutus with a touch of wistfulness. "To protect me when this plane turns into a big fireball and falls from the sky like a burning rock."

"Max?" said Dooley, a note of panic in his voice.

I gave him what I hoped was a look of reassurance, though to be quite frank I was starting to feel a little worried, too. The word picture Brutus was painting about fireballs and burning rocks greatly perturbed me.

"Promise me one thing, Max," Brutus said with a sigh.

"What?"

"Never change. Never stop being a fatty."

I drew myself up to my full height, which was a little hard, as I was indeed strapped in like a sausage. "I'll have you know that I am not a—"

Just then, the plane listed, and the humans all yelped in distress.

"—Mayday!" a voice over the intercom suddenly crackled.

"Max!" Dooley cried. "This is it! We're going down!"

4

"This is Captain Mayday," the voice over the intercom repeated. "And I'm happy to announce that we're about to land at Van Nuys Airport. The weather is a balmy eighty degrees and the sun is still out in full force. I hope you enjoyed your flight, and on behalf of myself and my crew I'd like to wish you a great time out west."

"I think the cats panicked there for a moment," said Chase, glancing back to what he'd called the kids' corner before.

Odelia had switched seats, since there was only so much of her grandmother's incessant nagging and needling she could stand. Clearly the old lady was in a lousy mood.

"Yeah, I don't think they'll ever be relaxed flyers," she said as she darted a worried look in the direction of her feline menagerie. "Maybe I shouldn't have brought them."

"Oh, they'll be fine. Not as fine as dogs, of course, but as cats go, yours are remarkably able to adjust themselves to new environments. Most cats hate to travel, and they hate going any place new and unknown."

"My cats hate to travel, too," she said, "and they hate new

places as much as the next cat, but they accept and adapt somehow." When she saw that her cats had settled in again, after their initial fright, she turned to face forward.

"Did Opal tell you what she needed you for?" asked Chase.

"No, actually she didn't." She patted the armrests. "She didn't want to tell me over the phone. She just said it was a matter of life and death, and that I couldn't tell anyone."

"Which is why you promptly told your entire family," he said with a grin.

She slapped his shoulder. "Opal said it was fine! The more the merrier, she said."

"Pity I can't help you with the case."

"Yeah, pity," she agreed.

Next to Chase, Uncle Alec suddenly woke up with a loud snort, and looked around confusedly. "Are we there yet?" he asked.

"Almost," said Odelia. "You better put on your seatbelt, Uncle Alec."

"Uh-huh." He yawned cavernously, then stretched. "This is the first time I've slept on a plane. From now on it's just private jets for me. No more commercial flights ever."

"Yeah, me, too," said Chase. "This is a damn sight better than whatever the mayor's secretary had booked us on."

Chase and Uncle Alec had been scheduled to attend a conference in Los Angeles on 'Policing Communities in the Twenty-First Century.' They hadn't been particularly eager to go, but it had been the mayor's idea that his most senior officers should attend more trainings, seminars and conferences from now on. Uncle Alec thought it was a waste of time and money, but the mayor was the boss, so off they went.

"Maybe you could stay at Opal's guesthouse along with the rest of us?" Odelia said.

"No can do," Alec grunted. "The airplane tickets were refundable, but the hotel isn't, and the mayor would blow a gasket if I told him we were going to stay at Opal Harvey's place instead of at the hotel."

"Besides, the conference is at the same hotel," said Chase. "And Opal lives on the other side of town."

"A very big town, I might add," said Uncle Alec, clicking his seatbelt buckle into place.

"Yeah, it would take us forever to get across town. LA is notoriously congested."

"And we might as well mingle with the other conference attendees," Alec said.

"But we could meet for dinner," said Chase. "You could all come to the hotel."

"Let's see what Opal wants from me first," said Odelia. "For all I know she'll send me on a wild-goose chase to hunt down some missing relative or something."

"You think that's why she asked you?"

"I have absolutely no idea!" she said, throwing up her arms. It was mildly frustrating not to know what she was getting herself into. Then again, this was Opal. It wouldn't be something fishy or illegal. Or would it?

"Whatever it is, text me the moment you know about your plans, all right?"

"Of course." She wondered, not for the first time, why Opal had hired her, and not one of the no doubt hundreds of perfectly capable and professional private detectives in the LA area. Then again, all in good time. She simply had to trust Opal's judgment.

Mom turned. "Who is this kid sitting next to your grandmother?" she asked.

"And how old is he?" asked Uncle Alec.

"He looks about twelve," said Tex, joining the conversation.

"His name is Hank and he's Gran's new boyfriend," said Odelia. "That's all I know."

"Her boyfriend!" said Marge with a gasp of shock. "No way!"

"He's of age, though, right?" said Uncle Alec, who looked genuinely worried. "They're not going to arrest my mother for hooking up with some pimply teenager, right?"

"He doesn't have pimples," said Marge. "Not as far as I can tell. Nice, clear skin. What?" she asked when they all stared at her. "I'm just saying he has very nice skin."

"He's young, Marge," said Tex. "We had skin like that when we were young, remember?"

"No, I don't," she said sadly.

"He's young but not too young, though, right?" said Alec, still worried about his mother's reputation.

They all turned to look at the couple. Odelia had to admit Hank did look as if he belonged in school. "Um… I'm sure Gran knows what she's doing," she said finally.

"Check his passport," said Tex. "Just go over there and discreetly check his passport."

"Too late," Odelia said, pointing to the ceiling, where the intercom was spitting out another message from the pilot, and where the 'fasten seatbelts' sign was still on.

"Hank," said Uncle Alec, shaking his head. "Where does she find them?"

"At the stud farm," Tex muttered dryly, which elicited a snicker from Marge and a suppressed guffaw from Chase.

And then the plane suddenly banked left, and they were descending fast.

5

When we finally walked off the plane, I was feeling a little groggy from all the emotions we'd gone through. But at least we hadn't crash-landed on a desert island, and been forced to spend the rest of our lives talking to a ball on a stick like Tom Hanks. Two stretch limos stood waiting for us on the tarmac, and when the door of the first limo opened, who would emerge but the queen of daytime talk shows herself!

"Opal!" Harriet cried, who was a big fan.

"Opal!" Gran screamed, who was an even bigger fan.

"Opal!" all the others gasped, as they suddenly came face to face with one of the best-known faces in America.

Opal, wearing thick horn-rimmed glasses, opened her arms and was smiling a wide, radiant smile. She was wearing a kaftan, the sort of dress only she could get away with.

Even though I was pretty sure the hug Opal hoped to dispense was intended for Odelia, Gran jostled her grand-daughter out of the way, then threw herself into Opal's arms.

"I'm your biggest fan!" she gushed.

Opal produced a loud chuckle. I had a feeling this kind of thing happened to her all the time.

"This kind of thing probably happens to her all the time," said Harriet, voicing my exact thought. She looked a little shaky. Like the rest of us, she thought the fact that the captain's name was Mayday was a lousy joke.

Dooley, who was shaking even more than Harriet, his teeth chattering audibly, said, "I'm never setting paw on a plane again, Max. No, I mean it this time. It's scary!"

"It is scary," I agreed, and then suddenly found myself being lifted into the air and pressed to an outrageously ample bosom.

"And who do we have here?" asked Opal, then held me aloft, which is a tough feat to accomplish, as I'm not the lightest cat in the world. She managed it without flinching, though. "What a cutie-pie!" she cried. "What an absolute sweetie!" And then pressed me to her bosom once more. For a moment I experienced nothing but softness and warmth, and my heart melted, then I was down on the tarmac again, watching how one after the other Dooley, Harriet and Brutus were undergoing the same treatment.

"What an adorable bunch!" said Opal, clearly a cat lover through and through.

"They are," said a proud Odelia.

"Can I just say that you're a personal hero of mine?" said Marge, a hand to her heart.

"Oh, that's so sweet," said Opal smoothly. "But you know who should be your greatest hero? You, my darling! Yes, you!"

Marge grinned like a bashful teenager, her cheeks flushed.

"And you, too," said Opal, pointing to Tex. "Who are you, by the way?"

"This is my husband Tex," said Marge, feeling compelled

to make the introductions as Tex seemed to have lost the capacity for speech. "Odelia's dad. And this is my brother Alec. And that's Chase, Odelia's boyfriend. They're policemen, here for a conference."

Opal's face darkened, and the smile vanished, just as overhead the sun suddenly plunged behind a cloud. "I hope you didn't tell them," she said, addressing Odelia.

"I couldn't tell them anything as I don't know anything," said Odelia. "Why did you send for me, exactly?"

"In the car," said Opal, her eyes turning shifty as she took in her surroundings.

Dooley glanced around, and so did I, but as far as I could tell, apart from the present company, there was no one else around.

"The cops ride in the other limo," said Opal, and her tone brooked no contest, so Chase and Uncle Alec dutifully got into the second limo. "You're with me," said Opal, and disappeared into the first limo.

"I guess... we'll ride with you?" said Marge.

"No, you heard the lady," said Gran. "Cops in the second limo."

"But... I'm not a cop," said Marge.

"You're a cop's sister, which is just as bad. Now scoot!"

And Marge being Marge, she scooted, along with Tex, and joined her brother and Chase in the second limo.

Gran, meanwhile, had already disappeared into the first limo. She might be a cop's mother but wasn't going to let the chance of riding in a limo with Opal pass her by. And as we all hopped in, I saw she'd taken a seat right next to Opal, her new best friend.

Hank, whom everyone seemed to have forgotten about, filed in next to Gran, and Odelia and the rest of us all took a seat across from the threesome. The door was slammed shut by an unseen hand, presumably belonging to the driver, and then the car was easing into motion, driving so quietly it was almost as if we were flying across the tarmac.

"So what's this all about?" asked Gran, wasting no time.

Opal's face had taken on an expression of concern, and she now pressed a button, causing the partition that divided us from the driver to travel down, blocking whoever was on the other side from seeing us—or hearing us, I imagined. Mysterious!

Opal fixed Odelia with a grave look. "I'm under attack," she said finally in a deep voice. "And I want you to find out who's behind it."

"Under attack?" asked Odelia, immediately concerned. "What do you mean?"

"Someone is trying to kill me, Odelia. My car was sabotaged just last week, and my coffee spiked with poison only yesterday."

"Spiked with poison?" asked Gran. "So how come you're still alive?"

"Because I immediately tasted something was wrong—I have a very sophisticated palate—and I had it sent to the lab for testing. Cyanide. In my morning coffee!"

"My God," said Odelia.

"So why don't you go to the cops?" asked Gran, having adopted the persona of the hard-nosed reporter asking all the tough questions.

"Because if word gets out that I'm being targeted, my investors will get spooked, my staff will freak out, and my stars will get rattled and run to the competition."

"I'm sorry, but I'm one of your biggest fans," said Gran, "and if I were to star on one of your shows I'd rally round and do whatever I could to track this miscreant down."

Opal smiled. "Thanks…"

"Vesta. And this is Hank. Say hi to Opal, Hank."

"Hi, Opal," said Hank, and gave her a little wave.

"The thing is," said Opal, folding her hands in her lap, "that I'm currently going through a business overhaul. I'm actively looking to expand my business and I need new investors to accomplish that, as well as the trust and support of my old and most loyal investors. If word got out about these assassination attempts, they might get cold feet and pull out. Investors don't like trouble. And they sure as hell won't like it if the person personifying the brand is in any danger. If I die, the company could go under, and under these circumstances they'll never invest, which could mean that the company will fold."

"I thought you were, like, super-rich?" said Gran. "Can't you invest your own money?"

"I'm rich on paper—most of my capital is invested in my company. Oh, sure, I have some real estate, and if I sell I could raise more money. But the same principle applies: as soon as I start selling property, the investors will smell trouble and pull the plug."

"So you're in dire straits, huh?" said Gran. "Look, if you need money, I could lend you some. How much do you need?" She was already grabbing for her purse.

"How about ten million?" said Opal.

Gran gulped. "Are you nuts?"

"Yeah, that's what Harlan told me."

"Harlan…" said Odelia.

"Opal's boyfriend," said Gran. "Don't you know anything?"

"Harlan doesn't agree with me, by the way," said Opal. "He says I should go to the cops. But I can't. I worked too long and hard to let my company go belly-up, just because some nutjob out there has decided to draw a target on my back." She leaned forward and grabbed Odelia's hands. "Promise me you will catch this person, Odelia. Marilyn told me there isn't a case you can't solve—she says you've got the touch. You're the real deal."

Odelia gave the talk show host a reassuring smile. "Of course. I'll find whoever is behind this, Opal. You have my word."

Then Opal turned to Gran. "And please be discreet about it. No one can find out what's going on, you hear? Absolutely no one." She then leaned around Gran to give Hank a hard look. "That goes for you, too, buddy boy. Not a peep from you, understood?"

Hank took the straw out of his mouth and paused from sucking on his umpteenth milk carton. "A peep about what, ma'am?"

6

In the second limo, which followed closely behind the first one, the conversation had quite naturally turned to a single topic: Hank.

"Who the hell is this guy anyway?" Alec asked again.

"And who are his parents?" asked Marge. "Where does he live? What does he do?"

"I wouldn't worry too much about Hank if I were you," said Chase. "I'm sure Vesta will get tired of the kid soon enough. Just like that guy she used to date—what's his name…"

"Leo," said Tex.

"No, Dick," said Marge.

"Rock," was Alec's opinion.

"Well, whatever his name was, he's gone, and this Hank kid will befall the same fate. Just you wait and see."

"I'm not so sure," said Marge. "She seems to be very fond of him."

"She was fond of Leo, too," said Chase, "and Rock and Dick."

"I think she told me she's angry with Dick, because he

told her he was Beyoncé's choreographer but then it turned out he wasn't Beyoncé's choreographer at all."

"Dick explained all that to me," said Tex, who happened to be Dick Bernstein's doctor. "He never told her he was Beyoncé's choreographer. That was a misunderstanding. He said he wouldn't mind being Beyoncé's *oceanographer* if she decides to take that trip around the world with her family the newspapers have been writing about."

"Oh, that's right. Dick used to be an oceanographer," said Marge.

"It was all just a big misunderstanding," said Tex. "And Dick has apologized but Vesta being Vesta she's refusing to even talk to him—or Rock, who she feels is also to blame because he should have told her Dick can't dance."

"Well, I just hope Hank isn't a serial killer," Uncle Alec grunted.

"He doesn't look like a serial killer," said Chase.

"And how would you know what a serial killer looks like?"

"Well, I've seen them on TV plenty of times," Chase said. "The impossible good looks, the blue eyes, the 'aw-shucks' goofiness." He paused. "Now that you mention it, you're right. Hank's got serial killer written all over him."

"Funny story," said Tex. "When Vesta introduced Hank to me just now I'm pretty sure he called her Vestal." When no one laughed, he added, "Vestal? Like in Vestal Virgin? No?"

"I don't care what he calls her," said Alec. "I just hope she doesn't wake up one morning to find that the little punk has cut her head off in the middle of the night."

"If he cuts her head off she wouldn't be able to wake up, though, right?" said Marge.

"True," Alec admitted.

And having exhausted the topic of Hank, they devoted the rest of the trip to wondering why Opal Harvey would have possibly hired Odelia. The general consensus was that she'd found a skeleton in her basement and wanted Odelia to figure out where it had come from—seeing as Odelia had gained some notoriety in that particular field.

They'd arrived at Opal's mansion, and as the limo zoomed through the gates Odelia glanced around and marveled at the beauty of her host's gardens. She thought she could spot a waterfall nearby, and plenty of greenery covering the large domain surrounding the main house, which, when it finally loomed up behind the bend, turned out to be more of a manor than a house. Built in Tudor style, with the exposed wood framework and the steeply pitched gable roofs, it could probably house not one but a dozen Opals.

"Finally. Home sweet home," said Opal with a contented sigh as the limo's tires crunched the blond gravel on the drive and eased to a full stop with nary a jerk.

"Nice place you got here," said Gran as she peered at the impressive building.

Opal laughed a full-throated laugh. "Yeah, it's not too shabby," she agreed.

Four cats eagerly sprang from the limo, and as they trod towards the house, halted in their tracks when the door swung open and a tiny ginger cat appeared on the steps.

"And that's my own precious Prunella," said Opal, a warm purr in her voice. "Contrary to you, I only have my one precious darling, but I love her to death."

"She must be quite old by now," said Gran.

"Can I let you in on a little secret?" said Opal, lowering her voice. "This is not the original Prunella," she whispered. "But don't let her hear it or she might get confused."

"What do you mean?" asked Gran. "She looks like Prunella. And I would know. I've been following your show since the very first episode."

"And when was the first episode aired? Do you remember, Vesta?"

"Um… twenty, twenty-five years ago or thereabouts?"

"Try twenty-nine. And when that show aired I'd already had Prunella for ten years."

"Which would make her…" Gran did a few quick calculations in her head. "Um…"

"Thirty-nine," Odelia finally supplied.

"Thirty-nine!" Gran exclaimed. "She looks really good for her age. What's the secret?"

"Cloning," said Opal with an air of satisfaction. "This is Prunella 2. When the original Prunella died, about fifteen years ago, I had her cryopreserved and cloned. The first clones didn't survive more than a couple of weeks, but this one, technically Prunella 16, not only survived but thrived. And she has the exact same personality my sweet, darling Prunella had."

Prunella now came treading down the stairs and sashayed towards them, her tail high in the air and not even deigning Odelia's own foursome a single glance.

"Oh, my sweet, sweet precious baby," said Opal, picking up the tiny bundle of fur and kissing the top of her head. "Are you happy mommy is home? Are you? Of course you are!"

The cat suffered the treatment stoically, and then produced a single meow.

"I'll bet she's hungry," said Opal. "Won't you all come in? I had dinner prepared."

The second limo, which had parked behind the first one, had already disgorged its passengers, and the small company now made its way inside, followed by four cats, who seemed less than excited to enter. The sight of Prunella had clearly put them off, and Odelia thought she could guess why. As lady of the manor, Prunella wouldn't enjoy welcoming intruders into her house, and cats can be quite vicious when unwelcome visitors trespass on what they consider their own personal territory.

"Don't worry," she said as she encouraged them to enter. "You're all welcome here."

"Prunella didn't look happy," said Dooley. "In fact she looked downright hostile."

"That's just your imagination, Dooley," said Odelia. "She didn't look hostile to me. In fact I think she's happy to know that you're all here to help her precious human."

"I'm not so sure," muttered Max, but they still followed her inside. A liveried servant closed the door, and when she glanced back she thought he looked about a hundred.

They were led into a large dining room, where the furniture was all dark mahogany, the chairs overstuffed, and the carpets high-pile and expensive. The walls were bedecked with pictures illustrating Opal's illustrious career. And as Odelia studied the glossy framed photos, she could see the road Opal had traveled from lowly local reporter, not unlike Odelia herself, to who she was now: one of the richest women in the country, and definitely one of the most famous and respected.

"Let's eat!" Opal cried, clapping her hands. "*A table*!"

Odelia happily complied, the rumble in her stomach indicating her body might still be on East Coast time, but her stomach was definitely ready for a West Coast meal.

7

As the humans sat down for dinner, we were led into the kitchen where presumably we could enjoy our own meal. At least if that fierce-looking feline would permit it.

One of the servants led us along a corridor and into a large kitchen that looked as if it had been built specifically according to Nancy Meyers's instructions. The movie director could have filmed her next picture there, possibly starring Meryl Streep or Diane Keaton, and she wouldn't have had to change a thing. Gleaming marble countertops, gorgeous wooden cabinets, two gigantic kitchen islands, and light streaming in through French windows leading out onto a stone terrace with wrought-iron table and chairs... Nice!

"The cats are here," announced the servant who'd accompanied us, and then promptly disappeared again.

Behind the stove, a woman was stirring a big pot. She was large and wholesome-looking, with cherry-colored cherubic cheeks. Next to her, seated on a kitchen stool, sipping a glass of some dark-colored liquid I suspected was port, sat a liveried middle-aged server. His cheeks were red, too, but not as an indication of health, but of the quantity of port he'd already imbibed.

"I don't like it, Helga," said the guy, frowning into his drink. "I don't like it one bit."

"Hey, that's your line, Dooley," I quipped.

"You're right," said Dooley good-naturedly. "He stole my line."

"Well, like it or not, it is the way it is," said Helga, still stirring that steaming pot as if her life depended on it.

"Don't tell them a damn thing, you hear?" said the guy, a note of menace in his voice. "Not a single word."

"My lips are sealed," said Helga.

"And you better tell that boyfriend of yours to keep his big trap shut. I'll know if he blabbed."

"Oh, don't be such a sourpuss, Hector," said Helga. "You know my George wouldn't breathe a word of what happened to that detective woman."

"Well, I wouldn't be too sure about that. He's always had it in for me, George has. And if he sees a chance to get me booted out, he'll take it—mark my words."

"Stuff and nonsense. George would never do that. Not if he knows what's good for him."

Hector looked up. He'd finally spotted us and heaved a deep sigh. "Cats," he said, proving he didn't miss a trick. "When will she ever stop taking in those horrible furballs."

Helga giggled. "They're not her furballs, silly. They're that detective woman's cats. Opal told me to take care of them as if they're her own. And that's exactly what we'll do."

"Oh, go on, then. Spoil them rotten. See if I care," said Hector, clearly a man who'd gotten up on the wrong side of the bed that morning.

Unless…

"Could this be the guy who poisoned Opal's coffee?" I asked the others.

"He looks like a killer," Brutus said. "He has that serial killer look."

"And how would you know what a serial killer looks like?" asked Harriet.

"I've seen them on TV plenty of times," said Brutus defensively. "The squinty-eyed look, the pinched face, the receding hairline. He's got serial killer written all over him."

"He could be the one," Dooley said as he studied this Hector fellow, who was now draining his glass of port and then legged it out of the kitchen and into the corridor, presumably to return to his duties, whatever they were.

"Who better to put cyanide in a person's coffee than someone with access to the kitchen?" I said. "And he could easily have sabotaged Opal's car, too."

"We'll have to tell Odelia," said Dooley. "She'll know what to do."

Just then, Prunella entered the kitchen looking as high and mighty as before.

We all went quiet, and I could feel the muscles in my hind legs tensing up, in full fight-or-flight mode.

"So who are you, then?" asked Prunella, allowing us the privilege of hearing her voice for the first time. She had a high and melodious voice. Very pleasant, I had to admit.

"I'm Max," I said, figuring I better make the introductions. "And these are Dooley, Harriet and Brutus. We're Odelia Poole's cats—the New York detective your human hired?"

"Oh, right." The cat paused for a moment, then said. "So who are you, then?"

"Um…"

She stared at me, clearly awaiting my response. "Well, Max," I said with a laugh, figuring she was having me on. "Like I said, Odelia Poole's cats?"

She stared at me, and blinked. "We have a very nice pool, thank you very much. Though I never go near it. Pools don't particularly appeal to me. I can't swim, you see." She smiled. "Well, then. This has been so much fun. Gave me a real appetite."

And to prove she meant what she said, she moved over to a large bowl which Helga had just filled with delicious-looking paté, and dug in voraciously. Within seconds the bowl was empty. Frankly I'd never seen anything like it.

"Yum," said Prunella. "That was nice." She then did a double take when she spotted me. "Hey, who are you, and what are you doing in my kitchen?"

"You're kidding, right?" said Harriet. "Max has already told you his name twice. Are you messing with us or what?"

"Yeah, are you messing with us?" Brutus growled, taking a step closer to the cat.

Prunella blinked again. "I don't like messes. Good thing we have Helga. She doesn't mind cleaning up any mess I make." She then licked her lips. "Say, I'm hungry." She glanced up at Helga, who gave her a bright smile.

"Hungry again, eh, princess? Come here, I've got just the thing for you." And she placed a large slab of fish on a plate.

"Yum," said Prunella cheerfully. "Watch me dig in." And she proceeded to attack the fish as if it was the first food she'd had in weeks.

"Now there's a good girl," said Helga with satisfaction.

Prunella, who'd been licking herself, suddenly seemed to notice us for the first time. She started violently. "Hey! Who are you and what are you doing in my kitchen?"

8

Dinner came and went, and so, unfortunately, did Chase and Uncle Alec, who needed to get to their hotel so they could check in and have a good night's sleep before their conference started the next day.

And then it was time for Opal to show her guests their lodgings for the night. Turns out they weren't staying in the main house—too conspicuous, Opal thought, in case her assailant was a member of her household staff—and to Odelia's surprise she'd relegated them to the guesthouse instead. But then when she saw the guesthouse, it didn't look like a guesthouse at all. For one thing, it was bigger than Odelia's own place and that of her parents combined. And for another, it looked as luxurious as the main house.

The guesthouse had originally been built so Opal's boyfriend, who was an artist, could spend the night there when he needed to be alone to ponder his art, which, according to the media mogul, used to happen about once a month. There were three bedrooms, and Gran immediately called dibs on the biggest one—the one belonging to the boyfriend.

Odelia was still not entirely sure she was the right person for the job, but Opal seemed to have complete faith in her, and that was good enough for now.

"If there's anything you need, just give me a holler," said Opal as she stood in the doorway. "Tomorrow I'm taking you to the studio. Bright and early, remember?"

"Bright and early," Odelia echoed cheerfully.

"Oh, and bring your cats, if you like. My staff are crazy about cats, just like me, and I'm sure they won't get bored down there. Prunella loves to tag along and I'm sure she'll make your fur babies feel absolutely welcome."

And then it was time to unpack and settle in for the night. The plan was for Tex and Marge to play the tourists for the next couple of days, while Odelia and Gran tried to discover who could possibly be targeting Opal. Marge had to be back at the library in five days, so that's all the time she and Tex had. Odelia hoped to have finished her investigation by then, and hopefully travel back together as a family, the same way they'd come.

Uncle Alec and Chase's conference would also last five days, so the timing was perfect—if she could crack the case, which was still a big if!

And as she lay in bed, four cats occupying the rest of the large four-poster, she stared up at the ceiling and tried to come up with a game plan. First things first. She needed to properly sit down with Opal and get as much information from her as possible about what had happened. Then she needed to talk to the members of Opal's staff, and find out what they could tell her. All in all, it definitely was a pleasant way to conduct an investigation.

"Odelia?" Max said.

"Mh?"

"I think we may have stumbled upon our first clue."

She sat up a little straighter. She hadn't paid too much

attention to her cats, having been busy unpacking and discussing her first impressions with her mom and dad and Gran. "What is it?" she asked.

"Well, remember how we got sent to the kitchen while you guys were having dinner?"

"Uh-huh."

"Well, we met Prunella—again—who's a very strange cat, by the way—and we also met a woman named Helga, who I think is Opal's cook, and a man named Hector who likes to drink a lot of port. And they were talking when we walked in and Hector told Helga not to say a word to you about something, and Helga said her lips were sealed."

Max looked at her expectantly, and she nodded thoughtfully. "Hector and Helga, huh? I'll have to speak to Opal about those two."

"So you think they did it?" asked Dooley excitedly. "Do you think they're the people trying to kill Opal?"

"I'm not sure, Dooley. I'll have to find out more to be certain. But it's definitely a very important clue, so thank you for that."

"I think Prunella is nuts," said Harriet.

"What makes you say that?"

"For one thing, she can't stop eating, and for another, she kept forgetting who we were."

"Yeah, she kept asking us what we were doing in her kitchen," said Brutus. "Even though Max had introduced us, like, five seconds before. I think there's something wrong with her wiring or something."

"Well, Opal told me that Prunella is a clone," said Odelia. "So maybe that has got something to do with it."

"A clone?" asked Dooley, perking up. "What's a clone?"

"Prunella was Opal's sweetheart—the original Prunella, I mean—and she loved her very much. So when Prunella died fifteen years ago, Opal was so sad she decided to have

Prunella cloned at a lab that specializes in that sort of thing. They basically made a new Prunella out of the old one."

"Oh my God," Harriet muttered. "That's too weird."

"Yeah, it is a little weird," Odelia agreed. "But Opal says the new Prunella is the spitting image of the old Prunella, with the same mannerisms and the exact same sunny disposition. She was telling us all about it over dinner. The original Prunella used to love having her belly tickled, and so does the new Prunella, and there were lots of other little things only a cat owner would notice, and she says it's almost like a miracle."

"Well, maybe it is and maybe it isn't," said Max, "but I think they forgot to clone a part of her brain, cause that cat? Isn't completely there, if you know what I mean."

Odelia smiled. "I think I know exactly what you mean, Max, and let's keep it between us, shall we? Opal doesn't need to know. She can't talk to Prunella, so she won't notice if she acts a little strange from time to time. Besides, maybe the original Prunella was exactly the same way. A little eccentric and a little absentminded."

There was silence for a moment while Odelia read a message from Chase on her phone and started typing her response. Then Dooley piped up, "Odelia?"

"Mh?"

"When we die, are you going to have us cloned, too?"

"Why? Do you want to be cloned, Dooley?"

He paused for a moment, then said, "Can I think about it?"

"Of course you can."

"I'll let you know what I decide."

"No way in hell am I getting cloned," said Brutus. "End up like that fruitcake? No way."

"We don't refer to other cats as fruitcakes, Brutus," said Odelia sternly. "That's not nice."

"Yeah, how would you feel if someone talked about you like that behind your back?" said Harriet.

"I wouldn't mind because I wouldn't know, would I?"

"Smart-ass."

"Try to be nice to Prunella," said Odelia. "She is your hostess."

"Oh, all right," Brutus grumbled, and put his head on his front paws. "But I still think she's weird."

"Yes, we've established that by now," said Odelia, and turned to switch off her bedside lamp. She felt a little weird herself, she had to admit. It was her first night in a long time sleeping alone again, without Chase by her side, and she was already missing him.

The light clicked off and the room was plunged into darkness. Then Max suddenly said, "It's really strange without Chase, Odelia. I miss him."

"Yeah, I miss him, too," said Dooley.

Harriet and Brutus agreed that they, too, keenly felt the absence of the burly cop.

"I miss him, too," said Odelia softly, gratified that her cats liked Chase as much as she did. But then she closed her eyes and soon sleep rolled over her like a warm blanket.

Meanwhile, on the other side of town, Uncle Alec and Chase were also missing something—the comfort of sleeping in their own beds, for one thing.

"This is just weird," Alec grumbled.

Next to him, Chase was feeling cramped. He was no small man himself, and lying next to the voluminous form of his superior officer in a bed that obviously wasn't made for two grown men of outsized proportions, he found he had very little wiggle room indeed.

"I'd sleep on the couch if we had one," he said.

"I'll bet the mayor did it on purpose," said Alec. "I'll bet he told his secretary to book us the smallest room in the hotel with the smallest bed. Just to get back at us."

"The mayor would never do such a thing. Would he?"

"Of course he would! Everybody knows the mayor hates my guts ever since I told him I didn't want Dolores replaced by a younger, prettier specimen."

"The mayor can't replace Dolores. She's the heart and soul of the precinct."

"Exactly what I told him. You know what he said? That we need to bring the Hampton Cove police department into the twenty-first century, and the only way to do that is by getting rid of old fossils like Dolores. He said that each time he walks into the precinct he almost gets a heart attack when he sees her grouchy mug staring back at him. A pretty young face would do wonders for our image. And he even had the perfect candidate."

"Don't tell me. That young niece of his?"

"Exactly! He wants her to get started at reception and rise through the ranks…"

"… until she's ready to replace you as chief."

"You guessed it, buddy."

"Well, it would make for a nice change to have a woman chief, Chief," Chase said with a grin.

"Over my dead body, son."

"Pardon my French, but you sound like an old fossil yourself, Chief. A dinosaur."

"I don't care! I'm going to stay in that Chief's chair until long after this lousy mayor is gone and been replaced with a decent one. A mayor who appreciates that a police officer doesn't have to look like a hot young model to get the job done."

"Did you just call the mayor's niece a hot young model?"

"Well, I guess she is nice to look at," the Chief admitted.

"I heard she's into older men, Chief, so if I were you I'd try my luck. Who knows, you might be calling the mayor your uncle soon."

Instead of responding, the chief merely grunted something that wasn't fit for print, and Chase laughed. In spite of the fact that he probably wasn't going to get a lot of sleep due to their peculiar sleeping arrangements, and the fact that he missed Odelia, he was still feeling pretty cheerful. But then the weight of running a police force wasn't on his shoulders. In fact there was no weight on his shoulders at all, since he had no cases to run, no suspects to pursue, and for the next five days there was nothing on his schedule except associating and fraternizing with fellow police officers from all across the country, swapping war stories and learning from the best of the best of the best. And even better: his sweetheart was in town, and any time he wanted to see her, he could.

And as his eyes drifted closed, he was still grinning.

9

The next morning, bright and early, Opal's limo took us into town, to the studio where her show was being taped. Opal's show ran daily on weekdays, and I was surprised to discover how many people worked behind the screens. I'd seen the show a couple of times—it was hard not to, with an avid fan like Gran—but it had always just been Opal on stage, interviewing people in front of a live studio audience. Well, her cat Prunella was usually there as well. She was a constant source of entertainment and something of a mascot for Opal fans. She usually sat peacefully next to Opal on her couch, but from time to time wandered off into the audience to go and sit on someone's lap.

I'd always figured the show was just Opal and Prunella doing their thing, but when we walked into the studio, the place was abuzz with activity, with literally dozens of people milling about. There were lighting people and sound people and props people and camera people, and when Opal took us backstage into a large conference room, I saw that there were half a dozen staff members sitting around the table, a large whiteboard on one wall, preparing that day's show. This was her team of writers and producers, and when Opal introduced Odelia and Gran, she didn't introduce them as two detectives, but as two new assistants-in-training being added to her team.

I think Odelia and Gran were as surprised as the rest of the team, and I could tell from the expression on Odelia's face she didn't know the first thing about writing and producing a daytime talk show.

Tex and Marge had accepted Opal's offer to be taken into town, where they planned to spend the day seeing the sights, and somehow I had a feeling they'd have a lot more fun than we would. I think Gran was already starting to regret insisting to assist Odelia.

Being carted around LA in a limo suddenly sounded like a lot more fun than sitting in this small conference room trying to come up with ideas for Opal's next show.

Harriet and Brutus had wandered off, and so Dooley and I decided to do the same.

"This place is huge," said Dooley as we returned to the studio where the show was being taped.

"Yeah, it's a lot bigger than I imagined," I agreed.

The stage looked just like it did on television, though without Opal there and no studio audience, it felt pretty empty.

People were rigging up lights and one person was vacuuming Opal's couch, paying special attention to the spot where Prunella usually sat.

After a while, we decided to get some fresh air. The studio was part of a larger studio lot, and there were plenty of so-called soundstages where shows were being taped. Some were talk shows, like Opal's, but some were actual television shows, and Opal had told us in the car on the drive over that big Hollywood movies were also being shot at the studio.

The studio lot was in Burbank, a part of LA where a lot of big studios are located, and as we wandered about, people passed us by riding in funny-looking little cars that reminded me of golf carts.

"Hey, isn't that Brad Pitt?" suddenly Dooley cried, gesturing to a man smoking a cigarette.

"I don't think so," I said, "unless Brad Pit has developed a stoop and lost his hair."

"He could have shaved it off for a movie."

"I doubt it. Brad Pitt wouldn't shave off his hair. His nice hair is part of his appeal."

"I guess so," said Dooley, disappointed. Part of the attraction of coming to LA is to see movie stars, and so far we'd only seen Opal, who was a star, but not really a movie star.

We traipsed on, and passed what looked like an Old West town. Two actors were recreating a fight scene. They were both dressed as cowboys and were pretending to shoot at each other, a director and movie crew standing around to put the whole thing on film. The set looked really real, with a saloon and a funeral parlor and a jail. Horses were drinking from a water trough, and as the men squared off, suddenly a large bag of sand dropped down from the roof of one of the houses and fell into the water trough. It spooked the horses who whinnied and neighed and then promptly galloped off.

"Cut! Cut!" shouted a red-faced man with white hair. "Who dropped that bag?! Idiot! Moron! Numbskull! You're fired! You hear me?! You'll never work in this town again!"

"They're not very nice here in Hollywood," said Dooley.

"I'll bet it's just that one guy," I said as we moved along. I didn't particularly like western movies, even when they were so obviously fake.

We wandered into an adjacent building, and soon found ourselves in what looked like a large hangar, big enough to house a plane, and it did: a real-life airplane standing at the center of this big hangar. All around, cameras were positioned, and next to the plane, a scene was being filmed. An actor dressed as an army captain sat kneeling next to an actor looking like a pilot. The captain was holding a gun in his hand and the pilot looked as if he'd just been shot. Presumably by the captain. The man on the floor was very pale, and had blood all over his chest.

"That man looks as if he's about to die, Max," said Dooley.

"I'm sure it's just makeup," I assured my friend.

"It looks very real," he said, sounding concerned.

"That's the point. If it looks real to us, it will look real to the people watching the movie."

"You were my best friend, Danny," the man in the captain's uniform said. "How could you do this to me?"

"I had to, Rafe," said the man on the floor, his voice raspy and weak.

"You didn't just betray me, you betrayed your country," said the captain.

"My country betrayed me, when they killed my parents and murdered my dog and slaughtered my cat."

"Your parents were Nazis, and I'll bet your dog was a Nazi, too, and your cat."

"That doesn't mean they had to kill them." A trickle of blood had appeared at the corner of his mouth, and his eyes now turned up in his head.

"It all looks very convincing," said Dooley next to me.

"Well, it should," I said, also mesmerized by the scene.

Suddenly, one of the people with the cameras looked up, and stared in our direction. He was a fat little man with no hair. He didn't look friendly. His next words confirmed this. "Cut!" he shouted, and I saw someone holding up a funny-looking board that read *Pearl Harbor III*. "Cut! Cut! Cut! What frickin idiot let those frickin cats in!"

"Uh-oh," I said. "I think we better skedaddle, Dooley."

"I think you're right, Max," said Dooley.

"Get those frickin cats out of here before I have a frickin aneurysm!" the fat man screamed.

So Dooley and I quickly scooted out the hangar door again, distinctly feeling we'd already outstayed our welcome. And as we made our way back to the part of the studio lot where Opal's show was filmed, Dooley said, "They're very rude out here in Hollywood, Max. Did you know they were so rude out here in Hollywood?"

"No, I didn't know that," I admitted.

"They use a lot of bad words."

"I guess they do."

"It's probably stressful to make movies."

"I guess it is."

"Still. That's no reason to use foul language."

"No, you're absolutely right."

And we'd just entered the building where Opal's production company was housed when a woman walked in and loudly demanded, "I want to see that horrible Opal Harvey and I want to see her now!"

10

"I need more emotion, people—more drama!" Opal said, tapping the table with her finger. She was seated at the head of the table, her team listening intently and jotting down notes on their smartphones and tablets. Odelia wondered if she was the only one who still used pen and paper. Gran, of course, didn't use anything. She just sat there, arms folded across her chest, looking grim.

"That guy over there looks like a real piece of work," she suddenly whispered in Odelia's ear as she pointed to a man whose hair was standing straight up as if he'd stuck his fingers in a power plug that morning. He also had an unnaturally pale pallor.

"It's rude to point at people," said Odelia, but she had to admit the young man did look suspicious. Then again, as her experience had taught her, it often wasn't the people who looked suspicious who were the culprits. It was the ones who looked harmless.

"Give me the long and the short, Suzy," Opal was saying. "What am I dealing with here?"

"Well, Miriam has been ridiculed in the media for selling

weird products on her website but nevertheless has garnered a large and loyal following," said Suzy, reading from her tablet. She was a roly-poly woman with large glasses and pigtails. "She divorced her husband, a famous musician, but stayed friends with the man in spite of the parting, mostly for the sake of the kids. She and her ex-husband and her new husband and her ex-husband's new girlfriend even took the kids to Cabo together so that's pretty special."

"That is special," Opal grunted, nodding. She wasn't taking any notes, Odelia saw, probably committing the whole thing to memory. "But where's the emotion? So far all I've heard is the media has always been mean to her, yadda yadda, divorce, yadda yadda, playing nice for the kids yadda yadda. But where does her story touch people's hearts?"

"I think we should bring the topic around to the kids," said the man Gran had deemed suspicious-looking. "I think the kids are the key here."

"I don't agree with Kurtz," a third person piped up, a young woman with a bobbing ponytail. "I think we should leave the kids out of this. Miriam has specifically said she doesn't want to talk about her kids. She just wants to plug her website."

"All the more reason to go after the kids," said the suspicious one with a horrible grin.

"No," said Opal, after her staff had argued back and forth for a while. "We don't go after the kids. That's not who we are. We want emotion, we want personal appeal, but we're not monsters, and if Miriam doesn't want to talk about her kids we'll respect that. But we don't want her to simply come on the show to plug her website either..." She thought for a moment. "Let's invite her mother. Let's make this a double interview and focus on the bond between mother and daughter."

"Miriam hates her mother," Suzy said. "They haven't spoken in years."

"Exactly! What better way to spice up the interview than to bring them face to face?"

"Are you sure she'll agree?"

Opal snapped her fingers. "Marcus, get Miriam on the phone. Right now. Tell her that if we can't have her mother on the show the interview is canceled."

"Yes, Opal," said Marcus obediently. He was a smallish man with a wispy little mustache and beard. He removed himself from the room to get Miriam on the phone.

"So what else have we got?" said Opal.

Odelia glanced around the table. It was hard to imagine one of these people could bear such a grudge against their employer they would try to kill her. And yet someone had.

Opal had sent them the files of all of the people on her staff, but so far none of them had raised any red flags. The trouble was, she couldn't exactly interview them and ask them straight out if they meant Opal harm. She needed to be discreet. No one was supposed to find out what was going on.

"I think they all look suspicious," Gran grunted. "They all look like serial killers to me."

"And how would you know what a serial killer looks like?"

"Bad hair, bad breath, bad attitude."

"In that case we're all serial killers."

Gran gave her the once-over, then sniffed her breath. "Yeah, you could use a mint," she said, "and a haircut, and you could be a hell of a lot nicer to your grandmother." She promptly got up and grabbed her purse. "I'm getting out of here. I have a headache."

Odelia decided to follow her grandmother out. They weren't exactly getting any wiser sitting in on this staff meeting, and she was getting a headache, too, probably from being cooped up inside an air-conditioned space with half a dozen bad-breath people.

Following her grandmother out into the hallway, she saw that Gran was making a beeline for the coffee machine.

"Great idea," she said gratefully as Gran handed her a cup of the brew and took a sip from her own.

"This show is quickly losing a lot of its appeal for me," said Gran. "I mean, it's one thing to watch it on television, but a whole nother thing to watch it being made."

"You never want to know how the sausage is made," Odelia agreed.

"More emotion, more emotion!" she mimicked Opal. "We're being manipulated by these bozos, you know that, right?"

"Yeah, I know."

"Poor Miriam. What did she ever do to deserve this? Mother-daughter bond, my ass. If I were her I'd flatly refuse to come on the show."

"I don't think these Hollywood people are in a position to refuse," said Odelia. "If they don't come on these shows, they don't get the kind of attention their movies need."

"The talk show circuit. I wouldn't want to be seen dead on one of these shows."

Odelia laughed. "Opal's biggest fan has fallen out of love with her idol."

"Oh, yes, she has," said Gran. "And it only took one meeting." She glanced around. "Where did I leave Hank?"

"He's probably wandering around the studio lot. Lots to see for a movie buff."

"Who told you Hank is a movie buff?"

"No one. I just figured..."

"Well, he is buff, of course. And he is *a* buff, too. That kid loves movies so much he wants to be the next Matt Damon.

Which is why I brought him along. He hopes to secure an agent while we're out here, so he's probably trolling their offices as we speak."

"How did you two meet?"

"We didn't. I hired him."

Odelia stared at her grandmother. "Come again?"

"You didn't really think a kid like Hank would fall for an old dame like me, did you? I pay him for his company. He's a gigolo."

Odelia almost choked on her coffee as it entered the wrong pipe. "A… gigolo?"

"Don't look so shocked. If men can hire a girl to keep them company, why can't I hire a guy? He's pretty good at what he does, and cheap. Just starting out in the business."

"But, Gran!"

"Don't you 'But Gran' me. At least Hank doesn't try to convince me he's Beyoncé's choreographer when he's not. Rock and Dick and the rest of those merry marauders? All liars and cheats. At least Hank will never lie to me. And he's very affordable, too."

Odelia was shaking her head. "Gran, really."

"Oh, come off your high horse, missy. Wait till you're my age and then we'll talk again. And don't you dare tell the others," she said, wagging a bony finger in Odelia's face. "I know what they're going to say and I don't want to hear it. Now how are we going to figure out which one of these jerks is the bad egg?" She was pointing to the conference room they'd just left.

"Frankly I have no idea where to begin. Unless…"

"Unless?"

"Max and Dooley overheard a strange conversation last night." In a few words she brought her grandmother up to speed on Helga and Hector.

Gran hit the palm of her hand with her fist. "That's it! It's always the servants that did it! The server sabotaged the car and the cook poisoned the coffee. Of course!"

"But why?"

"Who cares why? We got em—or the cats got them. Let's go and tell Opal now."

"Let's not. We're not sure they're the ones behind this thing."

"Sure we're sure!"

"No, Gran. Before I start throwing accusations around I want to be one hundred percent sure. What if they didn't do it? Opal will lose her faith in us, and the whole thing will get messy. I want to talk to this Hector and Helga before we break the news to Opal."

"Oh, all right. Have it your way, but I think you're too prudent. For all we know they could have sewn a bomb into Opal's kaftan which could detonate any moment now."

Just then, a loud voice hollered, "I want to speak to Opal! Opal! Are you there! OPAL!"

11

We followed the loud woman into the building, wondering what was going on. Security couldn't hold her, and she stalked down the corridor in the direction of Opal's offices.

"Opal Harvey! I demand to see you now!" the woman was yelling.

From different offices heads came poking out, and I was surprised to see how many people actually worked there.

"Opal has a lot of staff," Dooley commented, having come to the same conclusion.

"Well, she does run a website, a magazine and a show," I said.

"Opal Harvey! Show your face if you dare!" the woman was screaming. "OPAL!"

"Yes, yes, YES!" said Opal, suddenly emerging from the conference room, along with the rest of her staff. "What's all this noise?"

"You ruined me!" the woman said, stabbing an accusing finger in the talk show mogul's direction. "You did a piece on our farm and you ruined us!"

"I have absolutely no idea what you're talking about," said Opal. "Who are you?"

"My name is Jacqueline Jackson, and you did a piece on our dairy farm last month, how badly we treat our cows, and how horrible our milk is, and now no one wants to buy our products and we had to close down the farm. I demand retribution!"

"Well, if I did a piece on your farm I probably had good reason," said Opal, standing her ground.

"You had no right!" the woman screamed. She was squat and ruddy-faced, probably from screaming so much.

"Oh, you'll find that I have every right."

"I'll sue you! I'll sue all of you!"

"Oh, take a number, honey," said Opal with a shake of the head.

"You heard me!" the woman said, fixing the people surrounding her with a menacing glare. All of Opal's staff had now emerged from their offices. There were easily thirty or forty people standing there, taking in the surprising scene.

"I'll sue every last one of you! You work for a disreputable company and I'm going to make sure the world knows what's going on here!"

"Yeah, yeah, yeah," said Opal, clearly not impressed.

Security had finally caught up with the woman and now gently escorted her away.

"You ruined us! You did that, Opal! That's on your head!"

"Show's over, people," said Opal, clapping her hands. "Back to work, all of you."

"What was that all about?" asked Dooley.

"I guess Opal did a piece on that woman's farm and she didn't like it."

"No, I guess she didn't."

"Do you think she could be a suspect?"

"She could be. She certainly seems angry enough."

I could see that Odelia had the same idea, for she was already hurrying after the woman and the burly security guards escorting her out.

"Hey, wait up!" Odelia yelled, as she jogged after them.

"A woman in Opal's position probably has a lot of enemies," I mused.

"She does? But she seems so nice."

"Nice people can make enemies, too. Opal wields a lot of power. Every person she ever interviewed who didn't like the outcome of the interview could potentially be a threat. So how do we know who's the one?"

"I don't think she has enemies, Max. Opal loves cats. Cat people don't have enemies."

I wasn't listening. Instead I was following my own train of thought. "I'm sure Opal's security people have a list of all the people who ever threatened her," I said. "Let's tell Odelia to talk to them. It might be a wild goose chase but we have to start somewhere."

"Why would Odelia chase wild geese?" asked Dooley, but I was already off in search of Odelia. We finally found her in the lobby of the studio building, where she was seated in a corner, talking to the shouting woman. Security people stood nearby, keeping an eye out for trouble, in case the woman tried to accost Opal again.

"It all happened last year," said the woman, who looked a lot more sedate. She sat with shoulders slumped, and was close to tears now. "Opal's people visited our farm in North Dakota. We're the only farm that provides raw milk to its clients. A fully automated production line that cost us a fortune. High-quality milk that's very popular. People travel miles for our milk. We pride ourselves on our product, and we've been very successful, too. Until Opal did a number on us. We thought it was going to be a puff piece. You know, plug our farm and the health benefits of raw milk. Instead, it turned out she'd sent a spy to film what went on behind the scenes. Before we knew it, we were being accused of mistreating our animals. She even had our milk tested and claimed it was full of harmful bacteria. Which is impossible, as our milk is tested all the time, and nothing harmful has ever been found. Thousands of happy customers could have told her that."

"But she did manage to film your animals being mistreated?" asked Odelia.

"Well, yes, but that was one sick cow that was on the floor, waiting for the vet to arrive. They secretly filmed it just as it was in a terrible state—it had tripped and fallen and broken a leg. So while we were waiting for the vet to come, Opal's spy filmed it, and later claimed all of our cows were suffering the same fate. He basically accused us of being animal abusers, which is insulting and untrue. On the contrary. We love our animals, and treat them with attention and care." She shook her head. "It's so unfair."

"But why didn't you take her to court?"

"After the item aired all of our clients canceled their contracts, from one day to the next. We lost all of our business overnight, and since we work with very narrow margins as it is, it put us out of business. We're up to our eyeballs in debt, and we don't have the money to sue anyone. We had to sell our animals and close down the farm, and all because Opal decided that a bit about animal abuse would attract more viewers than a bit about an innovative way of animal husbandry and the benefits of raw milk."

Gran had also joined them, and now took a seat next to Jacqueline. "You know, I can't blame you for trying to take revenge," she now said, handing the woman a tissue.

"Revenge? What are you talking about?"

"You know, wanting to get even. If I were in your shoes I'd do the same."

Jacqueline frowned at Gran. "I have no idea what you mean."

"You're not going to let her get away with it, are you? You're going to make her pay, right?"

Jacqueline Jackson abruptly got up, then searched around for a moment. "Where are the cameras? I know you're filming this. You're trying to entrap me, aren't you? Trying to make me say things on camera and then use the footage to make me look bad again."

"No, I can assure you…" Odelia began.

"I know how you people operate. Everything for the ratings. Well, I'm done being used by you." And with these words, she stalked to the exit and walked out.

Odelia gave her grandmother a reproachful look. "Now look what you've done."

"What *I've* done? What you've done, you mean. You should have confronted her. Instead you just sat there and listened to her waffling on and on about her farm."

"You practically accused her of trying to kill Opal!"

"Well, she is the perfect candidate, isn't she? And I wasn't lying. If I were in her shoes I'd have done the exact same thing. Though I wouldn't have used cyanide. Too crude."

"Oh, Gran. You're a terrible detective."

"*I'm* a terrible detective? *You're* a terrible detective. I've only been here one day and already I've identified about a dozen possible suspects. In fact I'm starting to think this whole town might have it in for Opal. Maybe the question we should be asking ourselves is this: who here *doesn't* want to kill her?"

"I thought Gran was Opal's biggest fan?" Dooley said.

"I think she might not be her fan anymore," I said.

Oh, how fickle fame and fandom can be.

12

"Shouldn't you be paying attention?"

Chase muttered something, as he continued reading Odelia's text. "Odelia has already identified several suspects," he said.

"Good for her, but we're not here to solve Odelia's case for her," said the Chief. "We're here to learn about policing communities in the twenty-first century."

Chase put his phone away again. So far the conference was a bust. The person giving the keynote speech didn't just look like Rambo, he also was a big proponent of the Rambo method of community policing: go in hard. Let people know who's in charge.

"You need to show your citizens who's boss!" he was saying now, as he walked across the stage, clicking his little clicker device to show the next slide in his Powerpoint presentation. On the big screen behind him heavily-armed cops were seen pounding on people with big heavy clubs, and showcasing the kind of weaponry more commonly found on the battlefields of the Middle East. "You need to teach them to show respect!"

"I'm not bringing that kind of weaponry into my town," the Chief grumbled. Grenade launchers and automatic weapons were proudly hoisted up by cops armed to the teeth, behind them a vehicle that looked exactly like a tank.

"Imagine driving that thing around Hampton Cove. People would have my hide."

"The mayor will have your hide if you *don't* drive that thing around Hampton Cove," Chase reminded him.

The mayor was a big proponent of the militarization of the police department. He'd already told the Chief he was freeing up a budget to buy old army gear they could repurpose. The army, since it was pulling out of several battlefields in different parts of the globe, had combat gear for sale at rock-bottom prices, and police departments across the country were a primary market for that kind of stuff, eagerly snapping it all up.

"I don't want it," said the Chief stubbornly. "I'm not prepared to turn my police department into the military and my town into a battle zone. I'm a cop, not Rambo."

"No, you certainly don't look like Rambo," said Chase with a slight grin.

"What's that supposed to mean?"

Chase didn't speak, but merely gave the Chief's impressive belly a prod with his finger.

"I'll have you know I bought a Fitbit last week," said the Chief, and showed the little gizmo, which he had attached to his wrist.

"It's not enough to buy a Fitbit, Alec. You have to actually use it if you want to enjoy the full benefits of the Fitbit experience."

The Chief stared at the thing. "You mean…"

"You have to turn it on and start counting steps, or else it won't do a thing."

"Huh. Is that right?"

"Kingsley! Lip! Is there something you want to share with the rest of the group?!" suddenly the keynote speaker yelled. He was a buff guy, with a buzz cut and a take-no-prisoners attitude.

"No, sir, no!" the Chief said, blushing slightly when suddenly the attention of a hundred and fifty attendees turned on him. "We're good, sir!"

"You know what?" whispered Chase. "Let's blow the next session and go to the gym instead. They've got a great gym at the hotel. I checked it out this morning."

"The... gym?" said the Chief, his blush deepening.

"It's a place where you can do all kinds of exercises: machines, free weights..."

"I know what a gym is," the Chief grunted. "It's just that... I mean I don't know if I..." He patted his belly. "I'm not exactly in the best shape, as you've already established."

"So? Why not make today the first day of the rest of your life—a life filled with health and fitness?"

"Lip! Kingsley! This is your final warning!"

"I'm sorry, sir!" said Chase, holding up his hand. "Please carry on."

On the screen a tank was firing a rocket into a building, reducing it to rubble.

"Huh," said the Chief. "That's one way of dealing with civil unrest, I guess." He then heaved a deep sigh. "Okay, fine. Let's blow the next session and go to the gym."

For some reason he sounded like a man on death row, ordering his last meal.

"Okay, team, this is it," Opal said. They were all engaged in a huddle, just like on a football field, and Odelia found the experience quite enjoyable. She was cheek to jowl with the pale guy with the spiky hair called Kurtz, whom Gran had identified as a serial killer, and her other cheek was practically touching Opal herself.

"This is our time," Opal was saying. "This is our moment —our chance to shine. We're all heroes of our fate, makers of our own destiny, and the creative powers of a greater source are coursing through our veins, inspiring us—uplifting us—making us reach beyond our limitations and plugging into a higher power. Can you feel it?"

Murmurs of assent echoed through their little circle.

"I said, can you feel it?!" said Opal, louder now.

"Yes!" cried the serial killer.

"I do!" said Suzy.

"I can feel it!" said the bobbing ponytail.

"Let's pray," said Opal, and closed her eyes. "Oh, Lord, give us the grace to rise above our limitations and embrace an all-knowing, all-powerful, all-loving universe."

"Amen," murmured Opal's team, and with a loud yell they broke out of the huddle, and then it was time for the talk show queen to walk out onto the big stage.

Even from where she stood, Odelia could hear the roar of applause and cheers from the crowd as they greeted their famous hostess.

"I just hope no one tries to kill her while she's on stage," said Gran, whose cheeks were flushed. In spite of her misgivings, she'd clearly enjoyed this experience of being admitted into Opal's inner circle and going through her private pre-show ritual.

"Well, I just talked to the guy in charge of security and he confirmed that Jacqueline Jackson left the building and won't be admitted if she returns."

"Jacqueline isn't the only suspect, though, is she? I'm keeping an eye on that Kurtz fellow."

"I'm keeping an eye on all of them," said Odelia, who was

starting to subscribe to Gran's theory that there were probably more people holding a grudge against Opal than there were people who didn't.

"If there's a shooter in the audience..." Gran began.

"Impossible. They would never get a gun past security."

"Unless it's one of them plastic guns, the ones that can be printed with a 3D printer. They don't show up on security scanners."

Odelia heaved a deep sigh. "Let's just hope nothing happens. I don't want Opal to die on my watch. Well, I don't want her to die, period, but especially not on our watch."

"If that happened, I'm sure she'd kill us," said Gran acerbically.

13

Opal was clearly in her element. As she launched into her opening monologue, the crowd was laughing at her jokes, and it was obvious the woman was born to do this job.

"She's good, Max," said Dooley as we watched on. We'd found ourselves a prime spot to watch the show, where we were out of sight for both the audience and the cameras.

"Yeah, she certainly is," I agreed.

Odelia, meanwhile, stood chewing her bottom lip and looking particularly ill at ease. As a detective hired to protect Opal this was a tricky moment: the star was seated on stage in front of an audience of about a hundred people. Anyone could simply walk up to her and do her harm. Several security people were present, but Odelia was still nervous.

"The killer is probably up there," said Dooley, whose train of thought was clearly following my own. He was pointing to the series of booths behind the audience, near the studio's ceiling. "I once saw a movie where the killer sat in one of those booths with a sniper rifle," he added cheerfully. "Luckily he missed that time and Clint caught him."

"Not helping, Dooley," I said as Odelia's gaze now traveled up to the booths indicated and the chewing intensified. If this went on her lip wouldn't survive the onslaught.

"I'm sure the security people wouldn't let a sniper with a sniper rifle into the building," I said, and Odelia nodded, clearly on the same page.

"Oh, but this particular sniper paid off a member of the security team," said Dooley. "Very easy to do, and you'll never find out who it was they paid off to turn a blind eye."

"God," Odelia groaned, and suddenly took off, presumably to check out those booths.

"Now look what you've done. Odelia has gone off to find your sniper."

"He's not *my* sniper, Max. I didn't pay him to shoot Opal. Someone else did."

"We better go and help her," I said, and turned to follow Odelia.

I almost bumped into Harriet and Brutus, who'd suddenly materialized.

"Where are you going, Max?" asked Brutus.

"Dooley thinks there might be a gunman hiding in the rafters," I said.

"Oh, crap," said Brutus and both him and Harriet joined us in our hot pursuit.

We mounted a staircase and soon found ourselves in an area of the studio that obviously didn't attract the attention of the cleaning crew, as there were dust bunnies everywhere, and a sizable layer of grime and soot. It was also very hot up there. Not the best seats in the house, I imagined. Soon we were crawling higher and higher, and temperatures were rising. Finally we arrived in a narrow darkened corridor and I could see Odelia already opening the door to one of the booths located one next to the other.

As I joined her and took a peek inside, I saw lots of technical equipment, and a lone technician seated behind a panel with plenty of buttons and knobs and switches. He looked up when Odelia walked in, lifted his headphones and said, "Everything all right?"

"Oh, sure," said Odelia, giving him two thumbs up. "Just curious to see what kind of work goes into producing a show like this."

"Plenty of sweat and tears, trust me," said the guy, then let the earphones drop back onto his head and focused on what was happening down below on stage.

Odelia closed the door, and proceeded to the next booth. This one was empty, and only consisted of a couple of seats and monitors. Presumably so a producer or network executive could watch the show without being disturbed. There were two more booths, one of which held the guy in charge of the lighting, and one where three people sat staring at several screens showing different angles of stage and audience, and picking a different camera angle every couple of seconds. They didn't even look up from their job.

"No snipers," said Odelia finally. "Phew."

"Phew," Dooley echoed. "What a relief!"

"A lot of fuss for nothing," Brutus grumbled.

"At least we got to see what the show looks like from way up here," said Odelia.

And just as we were about to return down below, suddenly there was a loud scream. And as we looked down, I saw how a large section of the lighting gear detached itself from the frame holding it up and crashed onto the stage below, narrowly missing Opal!

"The killer is down there!" said Harriet.

Opal, who looked shook up, was escorted off the stage by two security people, but then seemed to reconsider and returned. "It's all right!" she emphatically spoke into the camera. "Just a little accident. I'm fine. Can you clean this up?" she asked, talking to a crew member who'd rushed onstage to deal with the mess. "We'll be good to go again in ten minutes," she said, quickly regaining her cool. "We're going to switch to commercials and then we're back. So don't you go anywhere." And this time she did walk off stage.

Odelia was already running down the corridor and then pounding down the stairs, followed by the rest of us. And as she burst through the door downstairs into the main area behind the stage, she wasted no time finding Opal.

"Ah, there you are," said Opal. "Let's..." She glanced around. "Let's go into my office."

She headed into the office, and Odelia allowed the four of us to sneak inside before closing the door.

"Do you see what's going on here?!" asked Opal, losing her composure. "That thing almost dropped on my head!"

The door opened and Gran entered. "What happened?" she asked.

"Opal almost got hit with a section of lighting rigged up over the stage," said Odelia.

"You mean like an accident?"

"That was no accident!" said Opal, pounding her desk with her fist. "Did you see anyone up there?"

"No, I didn't," Odelia had to admit.

"And where were you?" asked Opal, directing an accusatory glance at Gran.

"Little girls' room," said Gran, though I had a sneaking suspicion she'd gone in search of her boy toy instead, for I caught a glimpse of Hank just before we entered Opal's office.

"You should be out there trying to catch this guy," said Opal, pacing the room and looking very upset now. She placed a hand on her chest and sat down. "God, I suddenly don't feel so good. I-I can't breathe!"

"Here, let me get you some water," said Odelia, and filled

a paper cup at the water cooler located in the corner of the office.

"Oh, maybe I should just put the show on hiatus until this whole thing is resolved," said Opal as she took a grateful sip. "How can I possibly go on like this?!"

"It could just be an accident," said Odelia.

"That was no accident. They deliberately intended for that thing to crush me. A couple of inches to the right and that would have been my head. I missed my mark, you see. I always hit my mark but this time I missed it. If I'd hit it I'd be dead right now." She checked a big clock on the wall. "I need to get back out there. Commercial break will be over soon." She held Odelia's gaze with a pleading look. "Please find out who's behind this? Please, please, please?" And then she was gone, leaving Odelia and Gran reeling.

"Let's try and find out what happened," said Odelia.

And then they were gone, too.

"So now what?" said Harriet.

"Now we help Odelia and Gran figure out what happened," I said.

"I know what happened," spoke a voice from the door. It was Prunella.

"You do?" I said. "That's great. Please tell us."

"A banana," said Prunella.

I frowned. "A banana?"

"I know bananas are not ordinarily associated with cats but for some reason I suddenly have this incredible craving for a banana. Don't you?"

"Um… not exactly," I said. "Though I can see where you're coming from," I hastened to add when her face clouded.

"I like bananas," said Harriet, trying to humor Opal's cat.

"Where can I find one?" asked Prunella.

"We'll ask Odelia to get one for you," I promised. "But

she's a little busy right now—trying to find out who just tried to kill your human."

The small ginger cat stared at me. "Someone tried to kill my human?"

"Yeah, they tried to drop a big light on top of her head," said Brutus.

"It's a miracle they didn't hit her," Harriet added.

Prunella frowned. "Um… I hope you won't think me rude, but who are you?"

"Here we go again," said Brutus.

"My name is Max," I said. "Remember? We met in your kitchen last night?"

"Of course," said Prunella vaguely, though it was obvious she didn't know us from Adam. "Well, if there's nothing else I think I'll take that nap now." And off she went, presumably in search of a place to take her nap. And possibly a banana, too.

"I don't like this cloning thing, Max," said Dooley as we walked out of Opal's office.

"No, I don't think I like it very much either," I said.

"She's nuts," was Brutus's harsh diagnosis. "This cloning screwed up her brain."

"You guys!" Harriet suddenly exclaimed. We all looked up in alarm. "I just thought of something!"

"What, what?" I asked.

"What if… we are clones, too?"

14

"Kurtz is coming over tonight," Opal announced on the drive back to the house. The talk show hostess had managed to finish her show for the day, but it had obviously taken a lot out of her as she now looked pretty exhausted. Odelia could only imagine how it would feel to be under attack, not knowing where the next hit would be coming from.

They'd had the heavy stage light checked for signs of sabotage but there had been no obvious indications it had been tampered with. Yes, it had somehow disentangled itself from the heavy steel bar holding it up but it was hard to say how this had happened. An oversight on the part of the people rigging it up? Or a faulty bolt that had come loose? Hard to know for sure.

The occupants of the limo were all uncharacteristically quiet as the fancy car ate up the miles, the driver expertly navigating LA's famously congested highways as he took them back to the house, located in the city's hills.

It was Opal's safe haven. The home she returned to every

night to recharge her batteries. Where she could be truly herself, unencumbered by the weight of fame and the expectations of a global audience and legions of adoring fans.

"I don't know how long I can keep on doing this," she said now, as she leaned back against the headrest, her eyes closed and a deep thought groove dividing her brows.

"You mean…" Odelia began.

"I don't know if I can keep doing the show with this kind of thing hanging over me all the time." She opened her eyes and fixed Odelia with surprisingly mellow brown eyes. "You have to find out who's doing this to me, Odelia. And fast. If by the end of next week this hasn't been resolved I'm going to tell my bosses at the network I'm done."

"But you can't quit," said Gran, who, in spite of the fact that her affection for Opal had taken a hit, obviously wasn't prepared to see her show go off the air just yet.

"I can and I will," said Opal, with the same forcefulness and decisiveness that were a hallmark of her remarkable personality and which had served her well in her meteoric rise to the top of the media landscape. "If this person isn't caught by next week I'm calling it quits. At least for the time being. I can't work like this. I can't sit there interviewing guests knowing any moment something might drop down on my head and that'll be the end of me." She paused and frowned. "You know, maybe that's all this person wants: to make me give up my show." She cut a glance to Gran. "So you think this could be related to that Jacqueline woman? The one claiming I ruined her business?"

"Could be," Gran allowed. "Or it could be someone else who feels you didn't treat them the way they should have been treated. Anyone who appeared on your show and now harbors a grudge."

"Maybe you could make a list," Odelia suggested. "A list of

people who made threats or filed a complaint with the network against you over the years."

"Like I told that Jacqueline person, take a number."

"That many, huh?"

"Honey, you can't do a show like mine and not make a couple of enemies in the process. There will always be people who don't like what you have to say about them, and who'll threaten you with legal action. But you're probably right. I'll make you a list."

"There's also some members of your staff I would like to interview," said Odelia. "Like your chauffeur, your cook, your butler—in fact I'd like to talk to all of them."

"I'll arrange it," Opal said, closing her eyes again.

She looked very tired, Odelia thought, and no wonder. As if the pressure of being the most sought-after show host wasn't enough, this whole thing had come on top of that.

She just wished Chase could assist her. But him being a cop Opal had put her foot down. No police, not even Odelia's boyfriend or uncle.

"What did you think of the show, by the way?" asked Opal, rubbing her face.

"Oh, it was great," said Odelia. She had to admit Opal had handled the Miriam interview brilliantly. Miriam's mother had indeed come on stage, and mother and daughter, after some initial awkwardness—had quickly been on a path to forgiveness by Opal's gentle nudging, and by the end of the show had even hugged and declared that all was forgiven. And even after the show had ended, they'd sat together for a long time, talking things through and patching up their fraught relationship. It was like a miracle.

"Yeah, that was pretty amazing," Gran admitted. She'd had her misgivings, but clearly they'd been misguided.

"I know what you were thinking," Opal said now.

"You do?" said Gran. "What are you, psychic?"

Opal laughed. "Oh, my dear Vesta, it was pretty obvious from the expression on your face. You thought I was inviting Miriam's mother just to boost my ratings. That I was going to go all Jerry Springer on her and provoke a fight with the mother. But that's not how I roll. And that's not the kind of show I host. On the contrary. I want to bring people together, not push them apart. I don't want family feuds, I want to mend broken bonds, heal hurting hearts, reconcile fractured families. The only reason I wanted Miriam's mother on the show was because I'd heard they'd had a falling-out, and I had a feeling I could get them to look each other in the eye and maybe put them on the road to reconciliation. You'd be surprised how much healing can be done if only people would simply sit down and talk. And that's exactly what happened today. No miracles. No magic. Just giving two people the opportunity to talk and see things from a different perspective."

"You should have been a shrink, not a talk show host," Gran grunted.

"It's a line of work I could have pursued, and something that greatly interests me, that's true, and my own therapist has given me a lot of inspiration and ideas for the show, something for which I should probably give her full credit."

They'd finally arrived at Opal's home, and as the car gently rolled to a stop, she heaved a sigh of relief.

"Finally. You won't believe how happy I am that we got here safe and sound." The door was opened, not by the driver this time, but by a man Odelia hadn't seen before. He was distinguished-looking, with his silver hair and his deeply tanned face. He was dressed in a polo shirt and corduroy pants and as he took Opal's hand to help her out of the car, she folded herself into his embrace and suddenly the formidable queen of daytime TV was crying like a baby, her shoulders shaking as she heaved big sobs. "Oh, Harlan," she said. "They tried to kill me again!"

Harlan directed a quizzical look at Odelia over his partner's head.

Odelia shrugged and returned Harlan's look with a helpless grimace.

15

We'd all been very quiet in the car, but the moment we arrived and the car door opened, we were out like a flash, and, as if by silent command, convened behind the house underneath the rhododendrons, where we knew we wouldn't be overheard.

That's the one disadvantage of being able to communicate with your humans: anything you say can and will be used against you if they happen to overhear your conversation, and this was one conversation we didn't want Odelia to overhear, or Gran.

"We have to thresh this thing out once and for all," Harriet said, opening the meeting. "All those in favor of digging a little deeper into this cloning thing, raise your paws."

Four paws went up, even Dooley's, even though he still hadn't fully grasped the implications of Harriet's theory. He asked the same question he'd asked back at Opal's studio. "But if we're clones of our original selves, wouldn't we be able to remember?"

"I'm not sure," I said. "Though I'd be inclined to think that we wouldn't."

"We need to talk to Prunella again," said Harriet. "She'll be able to tell us what she remembers from her previous incarnation as her original self."

Brutus gave a snort and Harriet looked up with the sort of censorious expression on her pretty face that she manages to pull off so well. "If there's something you wish to say please speak up now, Brutus," she said haughtily, "or forever keep your big trap shut."

"Have you seen Prunella? She can't even remember who we are, much less who she used to be."

"True," I said. "Prunella does seem to have some serious issues with her long-term memory—or her short-term memory—or both."

"We don't have those kinds of issues, do we?" said Dooley.

"No, I guess we don't," I said.

"So… maybe that means we weren't cloned?"

"But you heard what happened to Prunella, right?" said Harriet. "She wasn't cloned just once, she was cloned no less than sixteen times. This Prunella is actually the sixteenth iteration of the original Prunella, so maybe that's why she's acting so weird all the time. She's a clone of a clone of a clone of a clone—to the sixteenth degree."

"Or maybe she's just the sixteenth clone of the original Prunella," said Brutus. "Only the lab people who did the actual cloning will know for sure."

"That's why it's important we find this lab and find out if we, too, were cloned," said Harriet, returning to her original point, the one she'd made at the studio, when we were all still stunned by her startling revelation. If we were to know for sure if we were cloned or not, we needed to go back to the source: the cloning lab.

"Why don't we ask Odelia?" said Dooley, not for the first

time. "Or Gran. Or Marge? They'll tell us if we were cloned or not."

"No, they won't," said Harriet, also not for the first time. "Do you really think they'll tell us the truth? Of course not! If we were cloned the last thing they want is for us to find out about it. The same way a father who buys his kid a new goldfish when the old one is found floating in its aquarium one morning isn't going to tell them about it."

"Odelia would never lie to us," Dooley said.

"Oh, Dooley," said Harriet, shaking her head. "You are so naive. Of course she's going to lie to us, and with the best intentions, too."

"Well, *you* probably weren't cloned," Dooley told Brutus.

"And why not? Why don't I get to be a clone, too?" He seemed worried that he'd be left out of this cloning business all of a sudden.

"But... you weren't adopted by Odelia," said Dooley. "You were adopted by Chase's mother."

"So? She could have had me cloned."

"Let's not get distracted by these side issues," said Harriet. "Let's simply assume that we're all clones, and our original selves are in a lab someplace, kept on ice, just in case we need to be cloned again."

Her words plunged us all into a brief moment of shocked silence. It was hard to imagine my original self stuck in a lab somewhere, on ice, dead as a dodo, while I was hopping around out here, perhaps the umpteenth iteration of my own true self. I swallowed with marked unease, and when Dooley spoke the next words, I think he spoke for all of us—voicing the welter of emotions we were all experiencing.

"I don't like being dead in a lab somewhere, you guys. I don't like it at all."

"None of us like being dead in a lab, Dooley," said Harriet, "but if this is the case we need to accept it and move on. But before we can do that, we have to know for sure."

"And the only way to do that," Brutus continued his mate's train of thought, "is by talking to Prunella and finding out where this famous cloning lab is situated."

"And then going over there to take a look for ourselves," Harriet finished.

And as if she'd sensed our urgent need for her company, Prunella rounded the corner of the house and joined us underneath the rhododendrons—third bush from the left.

"Hey, guys," she said by way of greeting. "What are you doing?" Then she frowned. "And who are you, exactly, and what are you doing trespassing on private property?"

"We've told you this many, many times before," said Harriet. "We're your human's guests. Harriet, Brutus, Max and Dooley. And we're not trespassing. We're here with Odelia, the detective trying to find out who's trying to kill your human."

Prunella's frown deepened. "Wait a minute. Someone is trying to kill my human?"

"Yes, they are. They dropped a big light on her head this afternoon, remember?"

Prunella obviously didn't remember a thing, which probably was a blessing in disguise. "I'm hungry," she said suddenly. "Do you guys want to eat? Cause I do."

"Before you do that, though," I said, glancing at my friends, who all gave me the nod, "there's something very, very important we need to ask you, Prunella."

"And how exactly do you know my name?" asked Prunella. "And who are you cats? I've never seen you around these parts before."

"Oh, God," Brutus muttered.

"Look, who we are is not important," I said. "But what I'm going to ask you next is. The lab where you were cloned, could you tell us where it is? We have reason to believe we were also cloned, just like you, and we want to visit the lab to know for sure."

"Cloned? What are you talking about, unknown trespasser?"

"Well, you're not your original self, see? You're a clone of the original Prunella."

"Prunella? Who's Prunella? Oh, that's right. I'm Prunella. And who are you?"

"Let's try to focus here, Prunella," I said, starting to feel a little desperate. "Where is the lab where they cloned you? Just give us the name and we'll take it from there."

"God, I'm hungry," said Prunella, with marked cheer. "I think I'm going to have a bite to eat. Do you want to come too, strangers? I know I'm not supposed to talk to strangers, or invite them into my home, but I'm suddenly feeling rebellious. So let's break the rules and have some fun together! What do you say?"

"Oh, dear God, please beam me up now," was what Brutus had to say.

16

As Opal had promised, Kurtz dropped by the house later that evening, to discuss the events of that afternoon. Opal had decided to take him into her confidence, knowing that he wouldn't go blabbing either to his colleagues or—God forbid—to the media.

They'd decided to conduct the interview in Opal's study, which was located on the ground floor. And since Opal didn't want to influence her assistant, she'd decided that Odelia and Gran should talk to him alone. He might be her most loyal and trusted PA, but that didn't mean he wasn't still a little intimidated by her presence. The disadvantage of being an icon and a legend, she'd intimated, was that people were often so impressed with her they had a hard time overcoming their sudden bashfulness. She'd learned over the years how to put people at their ease, but it was still a social hurdle to overcome, even with her own staff, who'd known and worked with her for years and years.

"So, Kurtz, tell us what you think happened this afternoon," said Odelia once they'd made themselves comfortable in Opal's study. She'd taken the maroon leather couch closest to the window, while Gran had decided to remain standing, just in case Kurtz tried to attack her—she still thought he could very well be a serial killer. The PA himself was seated on one of the overstuffed chairs.

Opal's study had bookcases that reached to the ceiling, a large mahogany desk that dwarfed the rest of the space, and where presumably she ran her empire, and stained-glass windows that overlooked the grounds, where that waterfall still attracted Odelia's attention and she vowed, once more, to take a walk as soon as she had the chance.

"Well, I think someone sabotaged that light," said Kurtz, whose name was actually Jack Kurtzman but whom everyone seemed to call Kurtz for some reason.

"You think it was sabotage, too, huh?" said Gran, safely ensconced behind Odelia now and out of reach of Kurtz's presumable serial killer tactics.

The pale PA nodded six times in quick succession. "Oh, sure. No way that light could have dropped down of its own accord. Sabotage, no doubt about it. I talked to the gaffers and the electricians and they're unanimous: those lights are checked before every show, and they were properly rigged up. They said the bolts that held that particular light in place had been unbolted."

"Unbolted?" asked Odelia.

"Properly unbolted," Kurtz said with satisfaction.

"Meaning someone intended that big-ass light to drop on Opal's head," said Gran grimly.

"Yeah, it sure looks that way," Kurtz confirmed.

"Any idea who could be responsible?" asked Odelia.

"None—but I have to say that one of the electricians has a criminal record. I mean..." He held up his hands in a defensive gesture. "I don't know if it's my place to tell you this—Opal told me not to hold anything back and that I should tell you everything, even the smallest detail, no matter how insignificant, so that's why I'm telling you—but when this man was hired I brought his criminal record to Opal's attention and she decided to hire him anyway, so..." He arched a meaningful eyebrow, as if to say, 'I told her so.'

"And who is this electrician?" asked Odelia, grabbing her notepad.

"Serge Brimley. He was arrested a couple of years ago."

"What for? Do you remember?"

"Um... no, actually I don't, but he does have a criminal record, and he was the person who rigged up those lights. Just saying."

"Any idea if this Serge would have access to Opal's car?" asked Gran now. She'd emerged from behind the couch, like a turtle poking its head out of its shell, venturing a little closer to Kurtz, as if deeming him not as dangerous as she first thought.

"Um, yeah, sure. Opal's car is usually parked behind the building, so anyone who works on the lot would have access to it."

"We need to talk to Opal's driver," said Gran, and Odelia nodded. They needed to talk to a lot of people.

"How about Opal's coffee?" asked Gran, inching a little closer to Kurtz.

"Opal's... coffee?" asked Kurtz.

"Yeah, you know, the coffee Opal drinks. Would this Serge fellow have access to Opal's coffee?"

"Um... you mean at the studio? I guess anyone would have access to Opal's coffee."

"Was Opal's coffee poisoned at the studio or at the house?" asked Gran, directing her question at her granddaughter.

"The house."

"Mh. That complicates things."

"It sure does."

"Serge could have an accomplice."

Kurtz's eyes had gone wide as saucers. "Opal's coffee? Poisoned?"

"Yeah, didn't she tell you? Someone dumped cyanide in her coffee. Almost killed her."

"Oh, my God!" said Kurtz, bringing a slender hand to his face. "This is terrible! Horrible! Who would do such a thing? Opal is a legend. An icon. A living saint!"

"Sure, sure. Now don't you go blabbing about this to your colleagues, you hear?" said Gran sternly. She had now emerged fully from behind the sofa and took a seat next to Odelia. "This is all strictly hush-hush, you understand?"

Kurtz nodded and mimicked closing his lips with a key and throwing it away.

"On second thought, I don't think Opal ever told us where this poisoned coffee was served," said Odelia, thinking hard, "but I always assumed it was at the house."

"I have a feeling we've assumed a lot of things, Odelia, and I think it's time we stopped assuming and started treating this investigation the way it should be treated: by looking at the cold, hard facts and nothing but the cold, hard facts."

Gran was right. That afternoon's events had really shaken the both of them. Somehow the full import of Opal's predicament hadn't really dawned on Odelia. But now it had. That falling light had really driven Opal's point home: she was under attack, and her assailant wasn't fooling around. He or she meant business. They wanted her dead.

"Do you know of any other people who would wish your employer harm?" she asked.

"And who would have access to her car, her coffee, and the studio?" Gran added.

Kurtz had gone even paler than usual, if that was possible, and now looked white as the proverbial sheet as he contemplated these questions.

"Um… there have been studio guests who didn't like the way they were treated."

"Like Jacqueline Jackson?" asked Odelia.

"Well, Mrs. Jackson was never a guest on the show. She was merely the subject of a small piece we ran last year."

"Mrs. Jackson said Opal treated her unfairly. That she lied about an incident with a cow and that she ruined her business by supplying her viewers with a false report."

"I don't think Mrs. Jackson is completely honest," said Kurtz. "Did she also tell you that out of the hundred and fifty or so cows she and her husband had on their farm over a dozen had to be put down in the course of the last six months alone? And that the vet who worked for them was the one who approached us when he saw the way they were treating their animals? I was at the farm myself, and I saw firsthand the state those poor cows were in. Dirty stables, cramped spaces—there was a lot of suffering going on."

"So you were the spy she accused of delivering a biased report?" asked Gran.

"Yeah, I was the spy Opal sent in to take the measure of the Jacksons and their operation. And the footage I smuggled out was just the tip of the iceberg. I think it's safe to say we did those animals a big favor by shutting down that particular operation. The Jacksons are a disgrace to their profession and shouldn't be allowed anywhere near animal husbandry ever again."

"Interesting," said Gran, nodding. "So do you think Jacqueline Jackson or her husband could be behind these attacks on Opal?"

Kurtz thought about this for a moment, pursing his lips. "Um… well, I would love to say that they are, but I don't really see how. She couldn't have possibly unscrewed those bolts this afternoon. Someone would have noticed. I guess she could have done something to the car—depending on what exactly it is that you think she did, and as far as the coffee is concerned..." He shook his head. "I'd say it's doubtful. Unless the Jacksons have a person on the inside, of course. A person they pay to do all of these things."

"The same way Opal paid you to spy on them, you mean," said Gran.

He smiled. "Yes. They'd probably consider that poetic justice. In all fairness, though," he continued, serious once more, "I don't see them resorting to murder, just to get even with Opal. They may be cruel to animals but that doesn't necessarily mean they're also potential killers."

"Good point," said Odelia.

"They're desperate, though," said Gran. "And desperate people sometimes resort to desperate measures."

"True," Kurtz admitted. He was eyeing them keenly. "So you're both detectives? Pardon my impertinence but can I just say you don't look like detectives?"

"And what are detectives supposed to look like?" asked Gran, a little acerbically.

"Well, um... I guess... butch and... a little surly, maybe? Like Philip Marlowe?" He laughed. "I know this is probably very cliché, but it's just that... I've never seen a woman detective before, and definitely not one as pretty as you, Miss Poole." He seemed taken aback by his own words, for once more he clasped a hand before his mouth. "I'm sorry. This is probably one of those metoo moments I'll regret for the rest of my life, isn't it?"

"No, it's not," Odelia reassured him. "And thanks for the compliment."

"Yeah, thanks for the compliment," Gran muttered darkly.

Kurtz swallowed uncomfortably, though by some medical miracle he managed to do so without making his Adam's apple bob up and down. "Well, I hope you ladies find whoever is behind this. Opal is our heroine, and we want to keep her with us for a long time to come. She's not just a talk show host, she saves lives, she heals people, and mends broken hearts. She's a miracle worker—even more so than Dr. Phil or Oprah Winfrey or any of those other wonderful colleagues of hers."

Once Kurtz was gone, Gran and Odelia sat discussing the interview.

"Do you really think Jacqueline Jackson and her husband are behind this?" asked Gran.

"I doubt it," said Odelia, "unless, as Kurtz suggested, they have someone on the inside."

"I like this Serge guy for this. He had access and he's got a criminal record, which makes him the perfect candidate in my book. Plus, I have a bad feeling about him."

"You had a bad feeling about Kurtz," Odelia reminded her.

"Kurtz is all right," said Gran with a throwaway gesture of her hand. "He's a loyal soldier and would never harm a hair on Opal's head. No, we need to find out more about this Serge what's-his-face and the only way to do that is by contacting the police."

"But Opal told us not to involve the police."

"And we won't," said Gran with a sly little smile. "We'll contact Alec instead, who'll have a little chat with his friends at the LAPD and ask them to do him a small favor."

"Very clever of you."

"Hey! I'm not just some Philip Marlowe. I'm Vesta Muffin. Ace detective."

"Yes, you are," said Odelia, but then a knock on the door announced the next interviewee, so she hollered, "Push—the door is open!"

17

"Push! Come on, Alec. One more rep!"

Alec pushed and pushed but found himself incapable of completing one more 'rep,' whatever a rep was.

"I can't!" he squeaked, and let the heavy iron bar fall back onto its holder with a loud clanging sound. He was perspiring so hard he thought he might expire soon.

"Well done, buddy," said Chase, patting him on the shoulder.

Alec couldn't speak. He couldn't even move. He was sucking in big gulps of breath.

They were in the hotel's gym, and as it happened they were the only ones there, all the usual suspects probably in the conference room listening to Rambo teaching them about all of his Rambo methods for beating their fellow citizens into submission.

"Take a sip," Chase said, handing him a bottle of water. "Staying hydrated is key."

"Breathing is key," said Alec between two labored breaths.

"Yeah, I think breathing is overrated," said Chase with a

grin. "And? How are you feeling? Invigorated, right? So much energy!"

"Dead," said Alec, finally managing to drag his battered corpus from the bench where he'd done eight pushups of a very heavy iron bar with some weights attached at each end.

And as he started searching around for the sign that showed the way to the showers, Chase said, "Hey, you're not finished yet."

"Oh, I'm finished."

"We did chest, Alec. Now we do back, and then half an hour cardio."

"Cardio! No way!"

"Look, I'm not going to let you do anything too demanding, but at the very least you need to go up on that treadmill and walk for half an hour. Show your Fitbit some action."

"Walk for half an hour?" he asked. "That's all I have to do? Just walk?"

"Yup. But first we're going to do twelve reps on the back pulley machine."

"But I don't want to pull my back!"

"Just take a seat there," Chase instructed, like the hard taskmaster he was, "and grab those handles."

Alec, in spite of the fact that he thought he could die any moment now, did as he was told and grabbed for the handles Chase indicated. "Now what?" he said.

"Now you're going to pull those handles. Pull as hard as you can. Pull, Alec. Pull!"

"I *am* pulling!" Alec cried.

"Oh," said Chase. "Sorry about that. I forgot to switch the pin."

He pulled out a pin and shifted it somewhere higher on the stack of weights.

"Now try again. Pull! Pull!"

Alec pulled, and this time there was movement. "This is hard," he lamented.

"It's supposed to be hard."

"You actually enjoy this?"

"I love it," said Chase as he took a sip from his own bottle of water. "You can't beat the high you get from a fantastic workout. Well, maybe sex comes close, but nothing else."

"The high… from a… fantastic… workout," he panted as he shifted that weight stack for the twelfth and final time. "That's it," he said, shaking his head. "I'm officially done."

"You did great, buddy," said Chase. "Next time will be a lot easier. You'll see."

"Oh, no, it won't. I'm never setting foot in this torture chamber again. Ever!"

They walked over to the treadmill and Alec got on one as Chase punched a couple of buttons. The treadmill started moving and Alec started walking. Chase was right. It wasn't too demanding, and soon he was actually feeling almost human again.

Next to him, his friend and second-in-command had also mounted a similar treadmill and was now running full tilt, his feet pounding the rubber as if he'd never done anything else. Amazing, Alec thought as he watched Chase punish that machine.

"So have you heard from Odelia yet?" he asked, now that he had some oxygen to spare and suddenly felt predisposed to chat.

"Yeah, there was another attempt on Opal's life this afternoon," said Chase, grim-faced.

"No way! What happened?"

"Someone tried to kill her by dropping one of those big studio lights on top of her. By some miracle she escaped without a scratch."

"My God. Did she call the cops this time?"

"Nope. Still doesn't want to get the police involved."

"That's not very smart," Alec said, who was a big proponent of always getting the police involved. Just then, his phone chimed and he took it from his shirt pocket. "Speak of the devil," he said, and picked up. "Hey, honey. I just heard about what happened. Are you all right?"

"Yeah, I'm fine," Odelia said. "Pretty spooked, though."

"I can imagine. How is my mother?"

"Oh, she's all right. Anxious to get the bastard. Say, listen, I need a big favor. There's a guy I need checked out. His name is Serge Brimley. He's got a criminal record. Do you know anyone in the LAPD who could run a check? Pull his file and see what he's done?"

"Sure. I'll get right on it."

"No, you won't," said Chase next to him. "He's on the treadmill, babe, and he still has twenty minutes to go!"

"I can do my twenty minutes later," said Alec.

"No way, José. You'll do your twenty minutes now."

"See what I'm dealing with here?" he spoke into the phone.

"Do your twenty minutes, Uncle Alec," said Odelia laughingly, "and get back to me as soon as you know more, all right?"

"He's torturing me, Odelia," he lamented. "Your boyfriend is making me do things that aren't natural. Pulling things and pushing things and walking on strange machines."

"I'm sure he means well," said Odelia, a smile in her voice.

"No, he doesn't! He's trying to kill me!"

"Nineteen minutes!" Chase yelled. "Hoppity hoppity hop!"

"I hate you, Chase Kingsley."

"Keep this up and you're sleeping on the floor tonight."

Alec merely grunted something, and disconnected. He

hated this fitness thing. Whoever invented these machines probably worked as a professional torturer before they'd gotten into the fitness racket. There was simply no other explanation.

18

We'd finally come up with a plan of campaign. It was now obvious that Prunella was a lost cause when it came to divulging the location of the cloning clinic, and that we needed to pursue other options. It was actually Dooley who came up with the idea to search Opal's study instead. A woman like her probably kept records of everything, not just about her business affairs but her private affairs, too, and so there was bound to be some document or bill with the name of the clinic on it hidden somewhere in her study.

So having decided this was our next port of call, we ventured in search of it. And we'd traversed the halls of the big house Opal built when the man Kurtz came walking out of one of the rooms.

"That must be it," said Harriet. "He's Opal's PA, and must have been in a meeting with Opal."

Kurtz came traipsing down the hallway, and when he saw us gave us a goofy grin. "Oh, hey there, cats," he said. "I didn't know Opal had gotten a new batch of cats in."

"We're not Opal's cats," said Harriet a little prissily. "We're Odelia's cats."

But of course he couldn't understand her. He gave us a little wave.

"Well, toodle pip," he said, and then he was off with bouncy step.

"What's a toodle pip?" asked Dooley.

"Probably some Hollywood jargon," said Harriet. "Come on. Let's go!"

The door to the room we now presumed to be Opal's study was ajar, so we snuck in, and much to our surprise we found it occupied not by Opal but by… Odelia and Gran!

They were discussing the case, clearly having decided to go ahead with the investigation without our presence.

"They didn't even invite us to sit in on the interview!" Harriet cried, clearly annoyed.

"I guess they figure they don't need us," Brutus grumbled.

"They probably forgot," I said.

"Or couldn't find us, as we were hiding underneath the rhododendrons," Dooley said, quite sensibly, I thought.

"Well, I don't care," said Harriet. "If they think they can do without us, we'll show them we can do very well without them, too." She made a beeline for the big mahogany desk and hid underneath is. And since I didn't want to appear disloyal—or get into a big argument with Harriet—I quickly followed suit, and so did Brutus and Dooley.

There was a knock on the door and a man came in, followed by a woman. I recognized them as Hector and Helga, and they didn't look happy to be there.

"It's the evil Hector!" Dooley whispered. "Here to confess his crimes!"

"Or simply to be interrogated by Odelia," I said.

"Hector and Helga?" asked Odelia in a kindly voice.

The twosome confirmed that they were, indeed, Hector and Helga.

"Take a seat," said Gran in a much harsher tone.

The two did as they were told, and meekly sat down in the spot indicated. From underneath the desk we had a first-row seat where we could follow the proceedings.

"It has come to our attention," said Gran, once more playing bad cop to Odelia's good cop, "that you've been plotting something. And we would like to know what it is."

"Plotting something?" said Helga. "Oh, no, ma'am. I'm not into plotting."

"Me neither," Hector confirmed.

"You were overheard talking to Helga in the kitchen yesterday," said Gran. "You said—and this is a direct quote—'Don't tell them a damn thing, you hear. Not a single word.'"

Hector had turned a lighter shade of pale, and Helga a darker tinge of crimson.

"Odd," said Dooley, "how humans can change color like that. Like chameleons. Look, she's gone completely red, and he's white as a sheet."

"It's something to do with the blood flow to the face," I said. "Some people's faces drain of blood, while others get flushed with blood when they're nervous or upset."

"How do you—" Helga began, but Hector gave her a prod and she quickly shut up.

"You also told Helga to tell that boyfriend of hers to keep his big trap shut. And you said you'd know if he blabbed," Gran continued the prosecution's opening statement.

Helga produced a loud gulp, then cried, "I'm so sorry!"

"Shut up!" Hector said between clenched teeth.

"I know I shouldn't have done it!"

"Shut. Up!"

"I couldn't help myself. I told him where he could find it, I did. This is all my fault!"

"Helga!"

"No, I want to come clean, Hector. They have a right to know!"

"No, they don't."

"I knew you were the ones!" said Gran. "So you poisoned that coffee, didn't you?"

"Poison?" cried Helga, her hands flying to her face. "No, ma'am! I didn't poison no coffee!"

"Then what the hell are you talking about?"

"The wine!"

"Helga!"

"No, Hector, I want to come clean!"

"You promised!"

"I gave him the key, ma'am, I admit I gave him the key—but he drank it!"

"You drank it, too, you stupid woman," Hector blurted out.

"See! He's always calling me names! It's the drink, ma'am. It makes him do stupid things."

"Helga!"

"No, it's true. You shouldn't drink so much, Hector. You're a very nice person deep down inside but when you're drunk you turn into this, this... ogre!"

"Drink? What drink? What are you talking about?" asked Gran.

Helga bowed her head, and stared at her hands. "Opal keeps a special stash of her best bottles behind lock and key, ma'am, and she entrusted me with the key. Only me, as she knows I don't drink, and she also knows she can trust me."

"It's not Opal's stash, it's Harlan's," said Hector, "and he's got plenty more where that came from."

"It doesn't matter! It's not your stash to take, Hector, or George's."

"George?"

"My boyfriend, ma'am. So word got out about Mr. Harlan's secret stash, and the fact that I had the key, and so Hector and George started pestering me to give them the key so they could take a look."

"We didn't 'pester' you. You volunteered the information," said Hector, angrily staring at the ceiling even as Helga kept staring at the floor.

"So finally I caved—you don't know how convincing George can be, ma'am. And he told me that if I didn't show him Mr. Harlan's secret stash he would never speak to me again, and I happen to love that man, ma'am. One day I hope to have his babies—that's how much I love that man."

"Christ," Hector muttered.

"You love Harlan?" asked Gran.

"No, George!"

"Uh-huh." Gran looked puzzled, and so did Odelia.

"Humans," Harriet said next to me. "They're so weird."

"So I showed him the cabinet. It's right there, next to Opal's desk."

She suddenly pointed in our direction, and we all scrambled back, just in case we'd been spotted. But of course we hadn't, so we scrambled forward again, like soldiers crawling through enemy brush.

"And of course the moment I opened it, it was as if I'd opened Pandora's box. They kept drinking and drinking and drinking and I said Mr. Harlan is going to notice you've been raiding his liquor stash and who is he going to blame? Me!" She pounded her chest. "And of course that's exactly what happened. He hired two detectives and now here we are. I just want you to know, ma'am," she continued, looking up, "that I adore Opal and Mr. Harlan and I would never have done what I did if George and Hector hadn't cajoled me."

"We didn't cajole you," Hector grunted. "You were only too happy to dip in yourself!"

"One little sip, just to have a taste!"

"You're a hypocrite, that's what you are," said Hector.

"See, ma'am! This is the kind of abuse I have to put up with!" And promptly she burst into tears. "Please don't fire me," she said. "I love my job. I love working for Opal. And I promise I'll never do it again. And I'll pay you back all the drink that was drunk."

"Look, now she's gone completely white and he's all red," said Harriet, who'd been watching intently.

"It is weird," I agreed.

"Like a chameleon," Dooley repeated.

"I once saw Chase's mom turn green," said Brutus. "She ate a piece of sardine, went green, and the next thing I know she's hanging over the toilet making strange sounds."

"I once saw Gran's face turn blue," said Dooley happily. "She had something stuck in her throat and almost choked. Tex had to grab her and perform the hemlock maneuver. She spat out a potato and then turned from blue to red. It was the strangest thing."

"It's called the Heimlich maneuver," I said.

"That's what I said," said Dooley. "The hemlock maneuver."

"Look, we'll talk to Opal, all right?" said Gran, her expression having softened considerably.

"Yeah, we'll talk to Opal and Harlan," Odelia chimed in. "I don't think they'll fire you over a glass of alcohol that you secretly drank."

"More like two bottles," said Helga, wiping away tears from her round cheeks.

"Two bottles!" said Gran, emitting an incredulous laugh.

"Maybe three," said Hector, who was now also staring at the floor.

"We'll pay her back," said Helga. "We'll pay her back everything we owe."

"She can take it out of my paycheck," said Hector. "And George. Don't forget George."

Both Helga and Hector had gotten up and Helga's hand suddenly disappeared between her bosoms, before unearthing a small golden key. It was attached to a chain, which she now took from around her neck and handed to Odelia.

"Here. I betrayed Mr. Harlan's trust. I don't deserve to carry his key anymore."

"Maybe it's all for the best," Hector sighed. "Never put the cat with the milk is what my mam used to say," he added. "I'm truly sorry for any inconvenience I may have caused."

And with these solemn words, they both turned on their heels and walked out, leaving Odelia and Gran lost for words. Whatever they'd expected, it clearly wasn't this.

19

Odelia and Gran returned to the living room, where they were met by Opal and Harlan. They both looked up when they entered, clearly anxious to find out what they'd learned.

"Here," said Odelia, handing Opal the small golden key.

"What is this?" she asked.

"Oh, I think that's mine," said Harlan, taking the key from Opal. He was dressed in a very smart smoking jacket now, and looked as distinguished and handsome as before. He shared an uncanny resemblance with George Hamilton, Odelia thought, and wondered if that was what had attracted Opal.

"It's the key to my liquor cabinet," Harlan explained. "I gave it to Helga for safekeeping when you told me I should stop drinking so much, remember?"

"So why did she return it?" asked Opal, snatching the key back from Harlan's hands, much to the latter's disappointment.

"She and Hector came clean just now," said Gran, who couldn't suppress a grin.

"Clean? Don't tell me they're behind the attempts on my life!"

"They're behind the attempts on Harlan's liquor cabinet," said Odelia.

"Hector and George found the temptation of all of that liquor just sitting there too hard to resist, so they persuaded Helga to open the cabinet for them," Gran explained.

"And managed to raid your stash."

"Oh, no!" said Harlan, taken aback. Opal merely looked grim-faced.

"And I don't think Helga was as innocent as she claims to be," said Odelia with a smile. "I think she joined in quite eagerly."

"They drank my liquor!" said Harlan. "Of all the dastardly —" But Opal placed a hand on his arm.

"Let them finish, darling. So what's the upshot?"

"Well, as I understand it you're three bottles down of the good stuff," said Odelia. "Though to assess the damage I guess Harlan will need to do a full sweep of the cabinet."

"Give me that key and I'll go and check right away!" said Harlan, indignant.

But Opal held the key out of his reach. "It's fine," she said.

"Fine! They stole my finest liquor!"

"Well, someone had to. And I'm glad they drank it instead of you. I told you to get rid of your stash, not to keep it behind lock and key and appoint Helga its guardian."

"You told me to pour it down the sink. You do realize that those bottles are worth a small fortune?"

"Your health is worth more than a small fortune, Harlan," she said, giving his arm a squeeze. "It's priceless. Now do as you're told and get rid of it." She handed him the key.

"But..."

"Oh, just do it already." She shot him a meaningful look. "Or else I'll do it for you."

He hesitated, then handed her back the key. "You do it, darling. I don't think I can."

And with these words, he walked away. His back was ramrod straight, but there was something poignant about the way he left the room.

Opal shook her head. "I should have gotten rid of that stuff myself." And with these words, she walked off after her boyfriend, a set look on her face and clutching that key tightly in her fist.

"I think that liquor cabinet is going to be raided once more," said Gran.

"Yeah, one last time."

"And in the meantime we're still no wiser about who could possibly be behind these assassination attempts."

"No, we're not," Odelia agreed.

"What a case," said Gran. "What. A. Case."

Just then, Odelia's phone chimed and when she took it out, she saw that it was Chase.

"Chase—what's new?"

"Well, your uncle called in a favor from a friend of a friend, and your Serge Brimley was arrested for underage drinking at the age of sixteen—sixteen years ago. Nothing else since."

"Underage drinking? That's all?"

"Yup. As you can see, the man is a hardened criminal."

She sighed. "Oh, Chase."

"I'm sorry to disappoint you, babe."

"It's fine. We just excluded the cook and the server, too. They did have a secret, but it involved liquor."

"Just like Serge."

"So what happened to my uncle? Did you wear him out?"

"I guess I did." She could hear loud snores in the background. "Trouble is, the moment we got back he dropped down on the bed and fell asleep. And we only have the one single bed."

"Can't you just roll him over?"

"Tough. Your uncle contends in the heavyweight division."

"Well, you're used to pushing weights, aren't you? So push this one."

"Babe, I can bench press two-fifty, but moving dead weight around is beyond me."

"Did you just call my uncle dead weight?"

"As much as I love the guy, at this point I do."

She laughed and disconnected.

"And?" said Gran. "Serge?"

She shook her head. "Arrested for underage drinking sixteen years ago. I wonder why his record hasn't been expunged yet."

"That doesn't sound like the stone-cold wannabe killer we're looking for." Gran lifted her arms and dropped them again. "Day two and we're still nowhere, honey. Nowhere!"

"Oh, well. Tomorrow is another day. Maybe we'll get lucky." And maybe her cats would come up with a vital clue —they often did.

Chase stared at the inert form of Chief Alec. He'd already tried rolling him over but that risked dropping him to the floor, and he didn't want to do that to his friend and colleague. Shoving him sideways wasn't possible, because of his spread-eagle position and the friction of his clothes against the sheets. And then he got it. He took a firm grip on the sheet and started pulling. It worked: Alec nicely shifted along with it.

Unfortunately, the police chief chose this exact moment

to shift over to his side. And since he was on the edge of the bed by then, he simply plunged into the void, landing on the floor with a dull thud.

Amazingly, he didn't even wake up—just kept on snoring like a lawnmower.

"Thanks, buddy," said Chase, and dropped down on the bed and dozed off.

20

We'd been hiding underneath that desk for what felt like hours and hours and hours.

First Odelia and Gran had left the room, but then soon after, just when we thought the coast was clear, Harlan had come stalking in, followed by Opal. They'd argued back and forth about the liquor cabinet for a while, until Harlan had watched as Opal opened the cabinet, which was indeed located right next to the desk, and had taken out all of the bottles, and carried them out of the room, followed by a wildly gesticulating Harlan.

Then, even as I'd already started poking my head from under the desk, the door had opened again and Hector had come sneaking in, had taken one look at the empty liquor cabinet and had uttered a loud lament, then had moved off again. The same thing happened five minutes later when the cook entered. She hadn't cursed as loudly as Hector, but clearly hadn't been happy with the new state of affairs either. And when finally a third man had come sneaking in, this one a bespectacled specimen with a big red nose, and had cursed, I was pretty sure we'd just met the elusive George.

When he left, I had a feeling the endless passage of humans might finally have abated. I was right, for the next ten minutes nothing more happened to disturb the peace and quiet of the study, and so we finally emerged from our hiding place.

Hopping onto Opal's chair, and then onto the desk, I looked around, like a general surveying the battlefield. There were plenty of bookcases in the study, as seems to be typical for studies the world over, but nothing that screamed records or personal files.

"She probably keeps her files in these drawers," said Brutus, who'd also crawled up.

Unfortunately, cats are slightly handicapped in the sense that we don't open drawers with the same ease humans do. Still, Harriet gave it a shot, squeezing a nail into the crack and pulling. And she actually managed!

"Hurray!" I said, like a general spurring on his troops.

The drawer contained a large assortment of medication. Cough drops, pill bottles, a box promising a good night's sleep to be had by all, but no documents or secret files.

The other drawers revealed nothing about a cloning factory either.

Finally I turned my attention to the computer located on top of the desk.

I pushed the button to boot it up, and before long we were glancing at a large picture of Prunella staring back at us from the computer screen.

The computer was locked, though, and in urgent need of a password to reveal all of its secrets.

I tapped the letters forming the word Prunella, and snap! We were in!

"Great job, Max," Brutus grunted, in a rare compliment.

"I watch a lot of movies," I told him.

"And it pays off dividends now," he said with a smile.

Dooley and Harriet had also mounted the desk and now four cats stood side by side, staring at Prunella's face.

"Now what?" asked Harriet.

"Now we look for any files associated with cloning," I said, and called up the search window, then spelled out the word KLONE.

Nothing.

"I think clone is spelled with a C, though," said Dooley, who watches a lot of the Discovery Channel.

"No, it's not. It's spelled KLOAN," said Harriet.

"No, it's KLOWN," Brutus opined.

"I think it might be CLOWN," said Dooley.

"Let's try CLONE," I said, and promptly a file popped up. It was a PDF file and so I tapped the mouse button twice to open it. And there it was. Prunella's file. There was plenty of information about the original Prunella, and how the cloning people had managed to clone her fifteen times with no acceptable result before they'd achieved the impossible: a perfect clone—at least according to the braggadocio in the file.

"Perfect clone, my ass," said Brutus.

"What's the address?" asked Harriet, and I scrolled back to the beginning of the file.

"Thank God, it's in LA."

"Far from here?" asked Brutus.

"Call up Google Maps," Harriet demanded.

"How do I do that?" I asked.

"Oh, you silly cat. Here. Give me that mouse."

"Harriet knows her way around a mouse," said Brutus proudly.

"Yeah, I like mice," said Harriet. "They're easy to handle if you know what you're doing."

"I don't like mice," said Dooley. "Mice scare me."

I wasn't sure whether he meant real mice or computer mice, but we were too busy to delve deeper into the matter.

Harriet expertly showed us how to handle the computer and tame the program called Google Maps.

"There," she said, pointing at the screen. "There it is."

We all stared at the map she'd drawn up, mesmerized.

"Is that where they keep our original selves?" asked Dooley.

"Yes, it is," I said. "At least, if we were cloned."

"Cryogenically frozen," Brutus said.

"Cryo what?" asked Dooley.

"Cryogenically frozen. Basically means they pop you into a freezer."

"Like popsicles?"

"Yeah, exactly like popsicles."

We all let that sink in for a moment. It's a strange feeling to know that your original self is stuck in a freezer somewhere in the middle of LA, frozen solid like a popsicle.

"I don't think I like being a popsicle, Max," Dooley confessed.

"I don't like it either," I said.

"Me, neither," Brutus grunted.

"Oh, well. It could be worse," said Harriet.

"How could it be worse?"

"Odelia could have let us die and buried us in the backyard. At least this shows she cares."

"How so?"

"Well, this cloning business costs a lot of money. This shows that Odelia spent all of that money to have us cloned, which means she must love us a great deal."

"We already knew that, though, didn't we?" I said.

"Yes, but this..." said Harriet, scrolling down the document to the last page and tapping a number, "... definitively proves it."

We all gulped when we saw the price Opal had paid to have her beloved cat cloned.

"Odelia must love us very, very, very, very much," said Dooley.

"Yes," I said. "To the tune of fifty thousand smackeroos."

21

"Hank! Hank, where are you!"

"What is your mother doing?" asked Tex.

"I think she's calling for Hank," said Marge.

They'd had a wonderful day being chauffeured around LA by Opal's driver. They'd seen the Hollywood Walk of Fame, Rodeo Drive, The Getty... And of course Santa Monica Pier, the Venice Boardwalk and the Venice Canals. Though she hadn't seen Matthew Perry, as she'd hoped. Marge was a big Matthew Perry fan, and had followed the actor since his *Friends* days. In fact they hadn't seen any famous actors or actresses at all, even though they'd taken the Celebrity Home Tour, leaving the limo at the starting point.

"Now that you mention it, I haven't seen Hank for a while," said Tex.

"Me neither. He wasn't at dinner, and I don't remember seeing him when we got back."

"I'll bet he went into town and won't be back until he's seen all the sights."

"Hank!" Vesta was still yelling, as if calling her dog. "Hank, come back here!"

"Did Odelia tell you about what happened today?" asked Marge.

"Yeah, she did. Absolutely horrifying. I mean, who would want to try and kill a nice lady like Opal? Just look at all the good she does with her show, and all the charities she supports."

"She is a nice lady," Marge agreed. She had been watching Opal's show for so long it had become part of her life. "Probably someone who's jealous of her success."

"Or someone who's not all there," Tex said as he took a seat on the edge of the bed and bounced up and down on the thick box spring mattress. "I love this mattress, don't you? Almost as if we're staying at some posh five-star hotel."

"This is better than a five-star hotel," said Marge. "More like a six-star hotel."

"The Opal," said Tex, spreading his hands as if indicating a marquee. "An experience that will last you a lifetime."

"She could rent out this guesthouse and make a small fortune," Marge agreed as she placed her smartphone on the nightstand. She'd quickly checked TMZ, one of her favorite sites. She liked a bit of light reading before going to bed.

"She doesn't need to make a fortune. I'll bet she's a millionaire—or a billionaire."

"I think she's a billionaire. At least that's what the magazines are saying."

"And the magazines never lie," said Tex with a wink.

They both got under the covers and grinned like a couple of teenagers.

"So comfy," said Marge.

"So cozy," said Tex.

He reached for his copy of *Field & Stream* and she grabbed

her copy of *Star Magazine*, and moments later they were both engrossed in their bedtime literature.

"Hank!" Gran hollered somewhere outside. "Get your ass back here!"

In the next room, Odelia was reading through her notes. Her cats were all ensconced at the foot of the bed, and had been suspiciously quiet ever since they'd gotten back to the guesthouse. But since she was so engrossed in her notes she hardly paid attention.

So far they'd ruled out three suspects—well, four, if George was to be counted. Serge Brimley, Hector and Helga and George. And Opal said she vouched for her driver, whom they'd also briefly talked to after dinner.

In a thick Irish brogue he'd explained to them how the car had clearly been tampered with. The brake lines had been cut, and as they'd been rolling down the Hollywood Hills on that fateful day, he'd pumped and pumped the brakes to no avail, and had figured his final hour had struck. With dumb luck, and a screaming and panicking Opal in the back, he'd managed to steer the car up an incline that forked off the main road and it had come to a full stop without a hitch.

There must have been someone upstairs looking after him and his employer, for how else could they have survived such a harrowing incident? Later he'd confirmed that the brake lines had, indeed, been cleanly cut, but nothing that a good mechanic like himself hadn't been able to fix, and now the limo ran as nice and smooth as before.

He hadn't seen anyone lurking around the garage that day or the days before, and he would have noticed, as he kept a close eye on Opal and Harlan's collection of cars.

And an impressive collection it was, Odelia had been able

to ascertain for herself: old-timers but also brand-new cars like Maseratis and Bugattis and Ferraris. Harlan had a penchant for expensive Italian cars, and Opal indulged his hobby with a generous hand.

Odelia had come to the end of her notes and realized she wasn't any the wiser.

"Hank!" she could hear her grandmother scream. "I'm not telling you again!"

Hank hadn't been at dinner, and when Gran tried to call him her call had gone straight to voicemail. The guy had effectively disappeared. She hoped it wasn't related to the case, but had a feeling it wasn't. If Hank was a gigolo, maybe he'd found a better-paying client out here in LA who wouldn't be such a tough proposition as Gran.

It was hard on Gran, of course, for now she'd lost her companion.

"Has Gran lost her boy toy?" asked Harriet now.

"I'm afraid so," said Odelia.

"Too bad. I liked him," said Brutus. "He had a way with words."

Odelia raised her eyebrows. A way with words? Hank? She hardly remembered the sound of his voice.

"He told me I was butch," said Brutus proudly. "Said he wouldn't mind owning a cat just like me one day. That I complimented his tan and the chicks would really dig me."

So that was why Brutus liked him so much. She smiled. "So how have you guys been holding up?" she asked, realizing she'd been neglecting her cats.

"Oh, we're fine," said Harriet.

"Prunella has been acting a little weird, though," said Max.

"Weird, how?"

"Well, she keeps forgetting who we are."

"She's been cloned," Dooley explained.

"I know. I was the one who told you, remember?"

"Oh, that's right," said Dooley, looking puzzled.

"Do you think the cloning caused her brain to get scrambled?" asked Brutus.

"Prunella's brains are scrambled? Really?"

"Oh, yeah," said Harriet. "Absolutely scrambled."

"Well… Opal told me the new Prunella is just like the old Prunella, so…"

"So you think she was always like this?" asked Max. "Scrambled, I mean?"

"I guess so. Opal would have noticed if this Prunella was substantially different from the original one."

"Weird, though, isn't it?" said Harriet, giving her a strange look. "This cloning business?"

"Yeah, Prunella's original self is kept on ice in some lab somewhere," said Brutus. "And the new Prunella walks around with scrambled brains. Very odd, huh?"

"Yeah, I guess it is a little weird," said Odelia. "But if you consider that only the genetic material of the original, cloned pet is used, and that the puppy or kitten develops like all puppies or kittens develop: inside a host, it's a little less weird. The so-called new Prunella was born like any other cat, and even though genetically she is a copy of the original Prunella, that doesn't mean she will look *exactly* the same down to the smallest detail."

"She won't?" asked Dooley. "You mean they didn't put her through a photocopier?"

"Oh, no of course not," said Odelia. "You can't copy a living being. What they do is take the nucleus of a cell of the pet they want to clone, and insert it into an egg cell. They give it an electric jolt and let the host carry it to term. And hope the process is successful."

"Oh, so that's how it works," said Dooley. "Nucleus, jolt, egg…" He looked confused.

"It's a complicated medical procedure," she said. "Say, you guys are acting a little weird. Are you sure you're all right?"

"Oh, yes," said Max, grim-faced. "We're all perfectly fine. Fine, fine, fine."

"As fine as can be expected," said Harriet. "Under the circumstances."

"Yes, the circumstances are terrible," Odelia agreed. "What with Opal being attacked today. I just hope we'll be able to catch whoever is behind this before it's too late."

"Well, if anything happens to her, they can always have her cloned," said Harriet. "That way she can go on with her show indefinitely and no one will be any the wiser."

Strange. They were acting so strange. But then Gran came rushing in, panting slightly, and asked, "Have you seen Hank? I seem to have misplaced the boy."

"Have you looked in the main house? Maybe he arrived late and decided to have a bite to eat in the kitchen."

Gran tapped the doorframe and gave her a beaming smile. "Thanks, hon."

And she was off again.

"Don't go to bed too late, Gran!" she hollered after her. "We're leaving early tomorrow morning, remember!"

But Gran was already slamming the door.

"Well, sleep tight, you guys," she said as she placed her notebook on the nightstand and switched off the bedside lamp.

"Sleep well, Odelia," her four cats said in chorus.

Then she remembered something. "Oh, tomorrow morning we're all going into town. Opal has invited us to join her at her beauty salon and spa."

"Doesn't she have a show to tape?" asked Max.

"No, it's Saturday. No show on Saturday."

"Where is this salon and spa?" asked Harriet.

"Um… Hollywood Boulevard," said Odelia.

There was a momentary silence, then Max said, "We'd love to come."

"Great. I thought you'd like it. They have a pet salon, too, so we'll treat you to a nice massage and a pampering session."

"Whoopee," said Harriet without much enthusiasm.

Yep, they clearly weren't themselves. Then again, cats being cats, that's just the way they were sometimes. They'd be right as rain tomorrow, she was sure. And then she dozed off. Outside, Gran had resumed her cries of 'Hank!' but by then she was fast asleep.

22

The next morning Odelia was the first one up. She decided to go for a walk in the grounds, and get some of that fresh air these Hollywood Hills were so famous for.

She ventured out into the cool and crisp morning air and took in a lungful of the stuff, which made her feel so giddy she broke into a spontaneous run and didn't stop until she'd reached a little brook and crossed it, finally to reach destination's end: the small waterfall she'd seen the first night.

It was a beautiful spot, with a gorgeous view, the sun rising over the hills, and spreading its gorgeous rays across a sleeping world. She took a seat on a small wooden bench and took in the breathtaking scene. Behind her, the brook gurgled, next to her the waterfall burbled, and inside, her stomach grumbled.

All this running had given her an appetite, and she couldn't wait to sit down for breakfast.

One thing was for sure: Opal was the perfect hostess, and not just on her famous show, but in her own home as well. The first-class meals they'd been served were so delicious Odelia was already dreading the moment they'd return home and she'd have to cook again. She'd never be able to compete with Helga, who clearly was a master chef when it came to the work she did in the kitchen, aided by Harlan's liquor stash or not.

She stretched and yawned, and a voice behind her startled her out of her reverie.

"Beautiful, isn't it? This is certainly my favorite spot."

She looked up to find she'd been joined by a woman who looked vaguely familiar. And then she recognized her. "You're Marilyn Coyn," she said. "Opal's best friend."

"That's me," said Marilyn. "And you must be Odelia Poole. The detective."

"Reporter, actually," said Odelia. "I'm just an amateur when it comes to detecting."

Marilyn, who was a statuesque woman with refined features, took a seat next to her on the bench. "That's not what I heard. I heard you're a damn fine detective."

"I do my best," said Odelia modestly.

"Opal told me what happened yesterday. That must have been a horrible scene."

"It was. And a miracle she survived."

"Opal seems to be on the receiving end of a lot of miracles these days," said Marilyn. "First those faulty brakes, then the poisoned coffee, and now this."

"She told you about all of those incidents?"

"Oh, yes, she did. In fact it was me who told her to hire you."

"But… we've never met, have we?"

"No, we haven't."

"So how do you know so much about me?"

"I read a story about how you caught Chickie Hay's killer, and that impressed me a great deal."

Of course. The Chickie Hay case had garnered a lot of publicity.

"I loved Chickie," said Marilyn. "She was one of my favorite singers and a dear friend."

"You knew her?"

"Sure. She was a guest on my show a couple of times, and we became fast friends. She was a bright young woman, and didn't deserve to die."

She remembered now. Marilyn had her own show, and even though it wasn't as popular or famous as Opal's, it still attracted a fairly large viewership.

"Have you gotten any closer to finding out the truth?" asked Marilyn.

"No, not yet, I'm afraid," she was ashamed to admit. "We've gone through a list of suspects but so far haven't hit on the right one yet."

"You have to figure out what's going on, Odelia. I can't lose another dear friend so soon after I lost Chickie. I wouldn't be able to cope with the loss."

She nodded. "I'll find out who's doing this, Marilyn. You have my word on that."

"I know you will," said Marilyn, placing a hand on hers and giving it a tight squeeze. "That's why I recommended you." She got up. "Shall we return to the house? We have an appointment with a beauty parlor, remember?"

"Oh, you're joining us? That's great."

"I wouldn't miss it for the world. Dr. Kavorkjan is amazing. He'll make you look and feel at least a decade younger." She arched an eyebrow. "Which, in your case, will make you look like a teenager again."

Odelia laughed. She liked this friend of Opal. She was funny.

"Have you seen Hank?" Gran asked me.

I shook my head. "I'm afraid I haven't seen him since yesterday morning, Gran," I said.

"He didn't come home last night," Gran explained, looking pained. "And he's not answering my calls."

"He probably hit the town hard last night and is still out partying," I suggested.

"Possibly," she allowed, "but at least he could pick up the damn phone."

"Or he could have been hit by a car or been killed in a mugging," said Dooley.

Gran frowned at him. "Not helping, Dooley! Not helping!" she said, and walked off in the direction of the main house, presumably to have breakfast. Or to pester more people in her endeavor to find her lost boy toy.

The four of us were seated on a bench that had been placed in front of the guesthouse. It was a great spot to watch the world go by, and to keep an eye both on the goings-on at the guesthouse, and the main house. In other words: the perfect cat spot.

"Poor Gran," said Harriet. "She just got her boy toy and now she lost him again."

"That's what happens with boy toys," said Brutus. "Now you see them, now you don't."

"Is he a real boy?" asked Dooley. "Or is he a real toy?"

"He's a real person, if that's what you're asking," said Harriet, a little snappishly.

"But why do they call him a toy if he's a boy?"

"Oh, Dooley," said Harriet, who has a lot less patience than I have when dealing with Dooley's tendency to ask a lot of difficult questions.

"I'll bet he's gone off to become an actor," said Brutus. "This town is contagious that way. Anyone who comes here catches the acting bug within hours of their arrival. Maybe they came here to be an accountant or a plumber or a ballerina but soon after they get into town they all switch careers and become wannabe actors instead. I guess it's something in the air—or the water."

I'd never heard Brutus turn philosophical like this before, and we all stared at him in surprise.

"What?" he said. "I have deep thoughts, too, you know."

"I think it's because you were cloned, Brutus," said Dooley. "I'll bet the original Brutus never had deep thoughts."

"And how would you know?" said Brutus a little brusquely. "You probably never had a deep thought in your life, not the original Dooley, and definitely not this carbon copy."

"That's a mean thing to say, Brutus," said Harriet. "Apologize to Dooley."

"I'm not going to apologize for telling an obvious truth."

"He's right, you know," said Dooley. "I never have deep thoughts."

"That's simply not true, Dooley," I said. "You have deep thoughts all the time."

"Give me one example," Brutus said. "One example and I'll happily apologize."

"Um… well, like last night, for instance, when Dooley said humans can change colors just like chameleons. I thought that was very deep."

"That wasn't deep," said Brutus. "He got that from watching the Discovery Channel."

"It was deep," said Harriet. "Now apologize to Dooley."

"Never!"

"Or how you figured out that Brutus is cloned, because now he has deep thoughts and the old Brutus probably didn't have deep thoughts to save his life," I continued.

"Max," Brutus said with a hint of menace in his voice.

"Brutus!" Harriet snapped, and directed a steely glance at her mate.

"Oh, all right," said Brutus, rolling his eyes. "I'm sorry, buddy. I'm feeling a little grumpy this morning. All this talk about clones and cloning has got me on edge."

"But why, Brutus?" asked Dooley. "Why are you on edge?"

"Don't you see? Soon we'll get to meet our original selves, and discover that we are just a bunch of carbon copies. Doesn't that make you feel anxious?"

"No, why?"

"I think I see what you mean, Brutus," I said. "If we are merely carbon copies of our original selves, it kinda makes you wonder if we're as screwed up as Prunella."

"Exactly! Maybe we're all as nuts as she is, and we simply don't know it."

It gave us food for thought, and when Prunella came traipsing up to us, and suddenly halted in her tracks and asked, "Who are you, and why are you trespassing on my territory?" the four of us shared a look of horror, and promptly burst into loud laments.

"I don't want to be a clone, Max!" Dooley howled.

"Me neither, Dooley!" I cried.

"I'm nuts. I'm a nutcase!" Brutus bawled.

"I knew it," Harriet sniffed. "I knew there was something wrong with me!"

"Oh, don't cry, strangers," said Prunella. "Eat a banana. You'll feel much better."

She was probably surprised that her words merely made those four strangers cry even harder. It's tough having to look in the mirror and realize you're a little screwy.

23

Immediately after breakfast, the entire company departed for Hollywood Boulevard, where the beauty salon and spa that counted Opal and Marilyn amongst its patrons was located.

In the limo, only women were present: Opal, Marilyn, Odelia, Gran and Marge. Tex had been left to his own devices, though Odelia was pretty sure he wouldn't be bored. Five cats were also present and accounted for. Prunella usually got a special treatment while her human got a special treatment, and she loved it, Opal assured them, and so would Odelia's cats. She didn't specify what this special treatment entailed, only that it was, well, special.

Opal was in excellent spirits, and had decided to forget about the harrowing events of the previous day and to enjoy this day out with the girls, as she called it, and have fun!

"So how long have you two known each other?" asked Marge, curious about the special bond between the two friends.

"Oh, how long, Marilyn?"

"Feels like a hundred years," said Marilyn, checking out a spot on her left hand.

"Thirty, thirty-one years? We were colleagues at our first-ever job. A local news network in Tennessee. That's where we met."

"I was the weather girl," said Marilyn, "and Opal had just been hired as a reporter to cover such fascinating and world-shaking events as the local bridal show."

"Or the pumpkin patch run," said Opal with a deep chuckle.

"We bonded over our mutual lack of a decent paycheck."

"And the way we were treated by the men in that place."

"It was a real boy's club," Marilyn confirmed. "The women were window dressing."

"The manager used to call us out for not showing enough cleavage."

"Can you imagine? Doing the weather forecast in a low-cut top? I felt like an idiot. And all of my family watching every day, and telling me I looked like a painted tart!"

"Not nearly tartly enough, according to the manager," said Opal.

"Oh, those were the days."

"And look how far you've come!" said Marge.

"Yeah, we did good," said Opal.

"You did a little better than me," said Marilyn.

"Oh, shush. You can't complain, Marilyn. You've got a top job at a top network. The kind of job only a guy would have landed thirty years ago."

"Thirty? How about fifteen years ago—ten, even."

"We broke through that ol' glass ceiling all right."

"And no low-cut tops required!"

Both friends laughed, and Odelia smiled. It was great to be in the presence of these two icons, legends in their chosen field. Gran, though, didn't look happy. At all.

"Have you been able to get in touch with Hank?" asked Odelia.

"No! He seems to have vanished from the face of the earth. I'm thinking about going to the cops."

"Oh, that boy is probably just having fun," said Opal.

"Or maybe he's been in an accident," said Gran. "Or been mugged."

"Or maybe he's having so much fun he lost track of time," said Marilyn. "Trust me, Vesta. I've seen it before. People arrive in town, cool as cucumbers, and before you know it they go completely loco. This town has that effect on people. It's a little like Vegas."

"Hank isn't the kind of guy to go loco," said Gran stubbornly. "He comes from a respectable home, and I promised his mom and dad I'd take care of him."

"His mom and dad? You told me you didn't know his mom and dad," said Marge.

Odelia was also surprised. "Yeah, you told me he's a gigolo."

Gran grinned. "I did, didn't I? And you should have seen the look on your face." Her grin quickly faded. "Of course Hank is not a gigolo, and he's not my boyfriend, either. I just said that because you can't keep your nose out of my business. Hank is Frank and Rita Peterson's son, and when I told them I was coming to LA they asked me to bring him along. Hank is working on his master's thesis about the movie industry and was dying to visit LA but couldn't afford it, so I told his parents he could tag along if he liked."

"I really thought he was your boyfriend," said Marge.

"Well, he's not. And let this be a lesson to you. Hank is a nice boy whose parents asked me to do them a favor, all right? And now leave me alone. I need to find him before they tear me limb from limb." And with these words she put her phone to her ear and was soon bellowing, "Hank! Pick up the phone! I'll tell your mom if you don't pick up!"

Alec woke up feeling stiff and store. He opened his eyes and wondered why the mattress had suddenly become as hard as a board. But when he looked around, he realized he was on the floor.

How had he gotten there? And what was that loud snoring sound?

He pushed himself up on his elbows and peered over the edge of the bed. Tangled up in the sheets, Chase was lying, snoring away, and occupying the bed's entire acreage.

"Oh, no, you didn't," said Alec, getting up. Before he could manage, though, pain shot through his chest and he plunked back down. "Owowowow," he yammered.

The snoring abruptly stopped and a face peered down at him. "Alec? You all right down there, bud?"

"No, I'm not all right!" he said, grasping his chest. First his left man boob, then his right man boob. "I have terrible chest pain! I think I might be having a heart attack."

Chase had the audacity to laugh!

"Hey, it's not funny! Better call a doctor. Or, better yet, call an ambulance!"

"It's not your heart, buddy. It's your chest muscles. How's your back?"

He moved a little, and excruciating pains shot through his back.

"It's radiating out to my back! It's cardiac arrest—I know it! Call an ambulance!"

"It's your workout, not your heart. You worked those muscles pretty hard yesterday, and now they're complaining about what you put them through."

"What *I* put them through! What *you* put me through!"

"Hey, you have to start somewhere. Here, let me help you up."

With a groan, and pain shooting through both his chest and back muscles, he got to his feet. "Owowowow," he cried. "That hurts."

"What you need is a hot shower and a relaxing massage," said Chase. "And you're in luck: they got both here at the Grand Continental."

"I hate you, Chase Kingsley," he said as he took a seat on the edge of the bed. "And why did you push me out of the bed?"

"I didn't push you. You fell."

"A likely story."

"No, really. And since I didn't want to wake you—"

"You decided to leave me lying on the floor. Nice!"

"Let's get you into that shower, and while you're soaking under that hot stream I'll book you a nice massage. How does that sound? And maybe we'll throw in a sauna."

"No workouts today?" he asked.

"No workouts today. I promise."

"Mh. All right, then," he grumbled, and shuffled towards the bathroom.

Ten minutes later, he was slowly starting to feel human again, his sore muscles gently massaged by the pleasantly powerful stream of hot water. And by the time he exited the walk-in shower, Chase announced they were both booked for a sauna at ten, and massages at eleven. "And no conference," Chase said sternly.

"We're playing hooky again?" Alec asked.

"Yep. Doctor's orders. I'll quickly pop into the shower and then we'll head down for breakfast, okay? At least," he said, halting in the bathroom doorway, "if you feel up for it."

The thought of that delicious breakfast buffet did much

to lift the police chief's mood. "I'm feeling up for it," he announced bravely.

"I thought as much," said his deputy with a cheeky grin, and disappeared into the shower before the spongy hotel slipper Alec aimed at his head could find its target.

24

We'd finally arrived at the beauty parlor, and the driver dropped us off at the back, so as not to attract any attention. We quickly hurried inside, presumably to thwart any attempts by lurking paparazzi or other lookie-loos to catch sight of us, and soon found ourselves inside the beauty parlor proper. It was a nice parlor, as parlors go, though I have to admit I don't have a lot of experience with beauty parlors, never having actually set paw inside one before.

There was a row of seats where presumably people had their hair done, judging from the sinks and the mirrors and the hair salon trays, a station where pedicures and manicures were executed, and of course there were tanning beds, a sauna, and even a hot tub where people could relax. All in all, a paradise for the ladies, but not for us cats.

At least not until we were led by a very kind-faced young woman to another part of the building, and suddenly found ourselves in pet paradise indeed: there was a play area where several pets were having fun with a multitude of toys in all shapes and sizes, scratching posts that reached all the way to the ceiling, a pet grooming station where currently a long-haired mutt was being relieved of his excess mane, and even a pedicurist devoted to those little pet nails, currently working on a Chihuahua.

"Pamper paradise," said Harriet, a little breathlessly.

"It's nice here," said Prunella. "I come here almost every week. It's basically a glorified waiting room for pets while their humans are gussied up next door, but I like it."

"I like it, too," said Harriet. "In fact I think I could live here."

"Aren't you forgetting something?" I said.

"What? Oh, you mean food? I'm sure they have a kitchen around here somewhere."

"We're not here to be primped and prinked. We're here to find our original selves in that cryogenic freezer."

"Oh, right," she said, clearly having completely forgotten about our special mission.

As luck would have it, the cloning lab and the pet salon and the beauty parlor were all part of the same operation. A one-stop shop, so to speak, where rich people could have their precious furballs pampered, but also cloned if they happened to drop dead overnight.

"Somewhere in this building is a cloning facility," I said, addressing the troops, "and we need to find it and figure out whether we were, indeed, cloned or not."

"Cloned?" asked Prunella, curious. "Are you cloned?"

"That's what we need to find out," I said. "Maybe you could help us?"

"Yeah, you've been here many times before," said Brutus. "Maybe you could show us the way to these cloning people?"

"I could help you," Prunella said, much to my elation, "on one condition."

"Of course. Anything," I said.

"That you finally tell me your names! I can't believe we've

spent all this time together and you still haven't given me your names." She tapped my chest. "Rude!" She tapped Brutus's chest. "Very, very rude, sir!"

"Well, I'm Max, this is Dooley, this is Harriet, and that black butch fellow over there is Brutus."

"Nice to meet you, Max, Dooley, Harriet and Brutus," she said pleasantly. "Now let's get going, shall we? Time and tide wait for no cat." And off she went, in the direction of the door.

Lucky for us, it was conveniently outfitted with a pet flap, and so we all slipped through in Prunella's wake.

"Keep up, keep up," she said as we tripped down a hallway and up a flight of stairs.

"I'll bet she's taking us to another playroom for pets," said Harriet. "She probably doesn't even know what cloning is."

"Maybe she will and maybe she won't," I said. I had faith in her, though, and had a feeling she was finally coming through for us.

And as we burst into a room located on the second floor, I saw that Prunella hadn't been kidding: she had been there before, and this place did look like a cloning lab, even though I'd never seen a cloning lab before. There were white-washed walls, though, and clean countertops with a multitude of instruments and test tubes, there were complicated and expensive-looking machines, and, finally, there was a wall of freezers near the back, and as we came to a full stop in front of them, we all took a deep breath.

There, inside those freezers, presumably rested our original selves. And now that we had finally arrived, I suddenly wasn't so sure I really wanted to know if I was in there!

There were several people working at their workstations. They were dressed like doctors, or lab technicians, in white coats, and all looked appropriately serious. They didn't pay any attention to us, though, probably used to working with animals all day long, dead or alive. One man was peering through a microscope and handling some strange device that looked like a pipette, dropping something onto a glass plate.

I returned my attention to the bank of freezers.

"So how are we going to find out if we're in there?" I asked.

"We're just going to have to open them all," said Harriet.

"And how are we going to do that? These are not desk drawers, Harriet. You can't insert a nail and pull. These freezers take a strong hand to open. A human hand."

"So? We'll simply ask one of these humans to open them for us."

I laughed. "Since when do humans listen to anything we say? Unless their names are Odelia, Vesta or Marge?"

"You said it, Max," said Brutus, gesturing to the door.

And as I looked over, I saw that Odelia was walking up to us!

"Oh, there you are," she said.

Shoot! She'd caught us red-pawed!

"The lab people told me you were up here. What are you doing sneaking off like that? Max?"

"Um… well, you know what cats are like," I said, going for blatant flippancy. "Always sneaking off and sticking their noses where they don't belong."

"We want to look inside these freezers," said Harriet, blowing my strategy straight out of the water. "We want to know if our original selves are located inside of them."

"Your original selves? I don't understand," said Odelia, frowning.

"She's just kidding," I said, laughing a laugh that sounded fake even to my own ears.

"They think they've been cloned," suddenly Prunella spoke up. "And now they want to find out of their bodies are in these freezers just to be sure whether they're clones or not."

Odelia started to laugh, but when she saw the serious expressions on our faces, immediately stopped. "You're serious? You really think you were cloned?"

"Yes, we do," I said.

"They took one good look at me and figured that if it can happen to such a gorgeous, attractive, intelligent feline creature like me, why couldn't it have happened to them?" said Prunella, suddenly sounding a lot less flaky than before. "Max," she added, "you weren't cloned. And I would know. I've been there."

"But... you remember my name?" I asked.

"Of course I remember your name. Even before you arrived at the house Opal already told me you were coming. You and your friends."

"But... you never remembered our names before," said Harriet.

"I was just messing with you guys," she said with a Cheshire grin. "And you fell for it, too!"

"But you *are* cloned, right?" asked Brutus.

"Of course I'm cloned. And the weirdest thing? I remember everything from my previous life *and* my current one. Hard to believe, huh?"

We stared at this peculiar cat, too stunned for speech, until finally Odelia crouched down and said, "Prunella is right. You weren't cloned. None of you."

"Is that the truth, Odelia?" asked Dooley anxiously.

"That's the truth, Dooley," she said. "Besides, apparently you would know if you were cloned, right, Prunella?"

"Hey, you speak our language," said Prunella. "That's something Opal didn't tell me."

"Can Opal speak our language?" I asked.

"No, she can't. I mean, she talks to me all the time, and of course I understand what she is saying, but unfortunately she can't understand me. Though after all these years we've created such a close connection she can feel me. Feel me?"

"Yes, I feel you," I said.

"So you see, Max? If you really were cloned, you'd know."

"What a relief!" said Brutus. "I'd hate to be cloned—no offense, Prunella."

"None taken," said the ginger cat. "Cloning is not for the faint of heart. No offense, Brutus."

"Um... none taken, I guess," he said.

"It's a strange and wonderful experience, and a little scary, but when you come out on the other side, it's great to know that you survived, and get to spend another couple of years with your precious human."

She was making cloning sound like fun, I thought, and clearly Harriet thought so, too.

"Can I be cloned when I die, Odelia?" she asked now.

"I don't know, honey. I'd have to give it some thought. Besides, you're not going to die any time soon, are you?"

"Oh, no. I intend to live a long and fruitful life."

"Me, too," said Dooley.

"And me," said Brutus.

"And me," I added my voice to the choir.

"That's the spirit," said Odelia with satisfaction. "And now let's get you back downstairs. These lab people get nervous when a bunch of cats suddenly invade the place."

I wondered why that was. They should have been used to us by now.

And as we traversed the lab, I watched on as lab technicians went about their business of creating new life. And I wondered if one day I might end up here, and emerge a new Max.

I shivered. Okay. So maybe not.

25

"I really had you going there, didn't I?" said Prunella cheerfully.

"Yeah, you really had us going there," I admitted.

"Do you even like bananas?" asked Harriet, "or was that a lie, too?" She didn't seem particularly pleased with the joke Prunella had pulled on us.

"Oh, no, I do like bananas. That was no lie," said Prunella.

We were back downstairs, in the pet playroom, and while Dooley was having his nails done and Brutus was getting a new coiffure, we were chatting amongst ourselves.

Odelia hadn't lied: we were there to be pampered and being pampered we were.

"I should be the one getting my nails and hair done," Harriet complained as she directed a jealous glance at Brutus and Dooley.

"All in good time," I said. "We're next."

"So you did remember this place?" I said as Prunella flicked a toy rubber ball.

"Oh, sure. Like I said, I'm in here all the time. Upstairs and downstairs. From time to time Opal takes me to the lab, so they can prod and poke me for a while. They tell me I'm their proudest achievement. I was one of the first pets to be cloned, and successfully, too."

"Well, I'm just glad it all turned out so well for you," I said.

"And for Opal," said Prunella. "When I died she was devastated, and when the lab people brought me back to life it was as if she'd been given a new lease on life herself."

"I wasn't kidding before. I want to be cloned, too," said Harriet. "How about you, Max?"

"I don't know," I admitted. "It's a little weird to think about that kind of thing."

And frankly I preferred not to think about it until I had to, which, I hoped, wouldn't be for a very long time to come.

"You know who comes in here all the time, too?" asked Prunella as she dug her claws into one of the huge climbing poles.

"No, who?" I asked.

"Kurtz."

"In the spa?"

"No, not the spa. They have the cloning facility, but they also have a clinic for humans here, where they do all kinds of surgical procedures."

"You mean like plastic surgery?"

"Uh-huh."

"Maybe Kurtz had his nose done?" Harriet suggested. "People in Hollywood have their noses done all the time."

"I know, Opal had her nose done last year," said Prunella. Now that she wasn't acting crazy anymore, she had turned into a real blabbermouth.

"Her nose? What was wrong with her nose?" asked Harriet.

"No idea. I liked it just the way it was, but apparently she didn't. It's much slimmer now. She had her boobs done, too, by the way."

"Bigger cup size?"

"Smaller cup size."

"Huh."

And while Prunella was spilling all of her human's most intimate and embarrassing secrets, Dooley came prancing up, then showed us his new and improved nails.

"Max!" said the girl responsible for Dooley's new nails. "Your turn, honey."

And then it was my turn to sit in the chair and have my nails done.

It felt strangely soothing, to be pampered like that, and I wondered if Odelia felt the same way. Probably she didn't. Odelia isn't the kind of woman who likes to be pampered. She's more the tough-as-nails reporter type. And tough-as-nails reporter types hate to be pampered.

"I love to be pampered!" Odelia cried, as she checked the pink-with-silver-sparkles gel nails her own nails had been outfitted with.

"Looking good, Odelia," said Opal, who was having her hair colored and curled.

"Now let's do your toenails," said the girl who'd talked her into getting the gel nails.

"Oh, yes, please," said Odelia. "This is so much fun," she admitted.

Though a tough-as-nails reporter like herself shouldn't enjoy this kind of thing, she actually did.

"Ooh, I want," said her mother when she spotted her new nails.

Mom had just had her face scrubbed and looked ten years younger.

"Tex isn't going to recognize you," said Gran. "You look like a new woman."

"I know, right!" said Marge, admiring her new look in the mirror.

Gran, meanwhile, was having her hair done. She'd hated the perm she'd been getting from her regular salon in Hampton Cove, and had been dying to try something new.

"You have to do Botox," said Opal now. "If you think you look younger now, wait until you get your first Botox treatment. It works wonders for your face."

"Oh, no, thank you," said Marge. "I'm afraid of needles."

"It's just a tiny little prick," said Opal. "You hardly feel a thing, and the results are astonishing. I'm not getting any today, as I just had a couple of shots last week, and I can't have too much Botox on account of the fact that I have a slight allergy to the active ingredient, but you should definitely have it. My treat!"

"Opal is right," said Marilyn, who was having her eyebrows done. "It's a miracle cure."

"Okay, maybe I'll try it just this once," said Marge, suddenly sounding giddy like a girl.

"Me, too!" said Gran, who seemed to have momentarily forgotten all about Hank.

"Odelia, I'm only doing this if you are, honey," said Marge.

"I'm not having Botox," said Odelia. "No way."

"Oh, come on, live a little," said Opal.

"You won't regret it," said Marilyn. "I promise."

"My treat!" Opal repeated. "Make that man of yours bug his eyes out."

Odelia giggled. She could just imagine the look on Chase's face when he saw her, all Hollywooded up. "Oh, all right," she said. "Why not?"

"That's the spirit," said Opal with satisfaction.

"Remember when we got our first Botox, darling?" said Marilyn.

"As if it was yesterday. I walked in this haggard, old person, and walked out a fresh young blossom."

"Well, not a young blossom, maybe, but looking damn good!"

"And now if you'll excuse me," said Opal as she relaxed in her chair. "I'm taking a nap."

A weird-looking device had been placed over her face, radiating a reddish light.

"Infrared lamp," Opal said, catching Odelia's quizzical look. "Works like a charm, but always makes me fall asleep." And to prove she wasn't kidding, soon she was softly snoring, eliciting snorts of laughter from the rest of the company.

Before long, Marge was having her first-ever Botox treatment, while Gran and Odelia relaxed in the hot tub. And Odelia was just thinking she could get used to this kind of thing when suddenly a loud scream pierced the laid-back atmosphere of the spa.

They both got out of the tub as fast as they could, slung towels around themselves and were already running in the direction of the screams when a second, louder scream startled them.

"That's Opal!" said Gran. "I'd recognize that voice anywhere!"

They hurried into the beauty parlor section of the spa, and found Opal writhing on the floor in visible pain.

"I'm so sorry!" a girl was saying, a needle still in her hand. "You should have told me you were allergic!"

"Get Dr. Kavorkjan! Get him now!" Opal yelled.

The girl hurried off in the direction of the clinic.

"What happened?" asked Odelia, kneeling next to the talk show host, who was clearly in a lot of pain. Her face was bloodied and swollen, and she looked as if she'd been attacked by a swarm of mad bees.

"Botox!" she managed between severely swollen lips. "They gave me Botox while I was asleep!"

Before Odelia's eyes, her face continued to swell, and her eyes swiveled wildly. Foam had appeared on her lips and she was making horrible choking sounds.

"Out of my way!" a man yelled and knelt down next to the stricken Opal. "She's having an attack," he muttered. "Call an ambulance. Call an ambulance now!"

And as he worked on Opal, Odelia did as she was told.

"She's going to die," said Gran. "This is it, Odelia. We lost our client."

26

We were all at the hospital, waiting for news about Opal. Even Uncle Alec and Chase had arrived, and Tex, of course, to see what could be done. In truth? Not much. Opal's fate was in the hands of the doctors now, and only they could save her, or not.

"Terrible, isn't it?" asked Harriet.

What was especially terrible was that the pedicurist working on Harriet had only finished three paws, which now left her out of balance, at least according to her.

"How could this happen?" asked Brutus.

"Apparently Opal has a Botox allergy," I explained, "and she had an overdose of the stuff, which caused her throat to swell up and her heart to stop."

"That's not good, is it, Max?" said Dooley. "A heart isn't supposed to stop, right?"

"No, usually it's not a good sign," I agreed.

"I think you can die when your heart stops," said Dooley, turning to Harriet.

"Oh, Dooley," said Harriet, shaking her head.

"Maybe we can have her cloned," said Prunella, who was

waiting with us in the hospital corridor. "But they'll have to hurry. They need to extract some genetic material from her before she dies and immediately start the cloning process."

"Cloning humans is not allowed," I said, trying to break the news to her gently.

"But why? If they can clone pets, why not humans?"

"I'm not sure," I said, "but I just know that no human has ever been cloned. At least not to my knowledge."

"I'm sure plenty of humans have been cloned," said Brutus. "The Nazis, for one, were already experimenting with cloning techniques in the forties, and so were the Soviets. So I'm pretty sure cloned humans walk among us, only we don't know it."

"I think cloning humans should be allowed," said Dooley suddenly. "Think about the great minds that could be preserved for posterity. Einstein, Marie Curie, Bell..."

"It's not the Einsteins of this world that will be cloned, though," I said. "Most probably they'll clone football stars and celebrities instead."

"But the world needs geniuses," said Dooley. "We've already got plenty of football stars."

"There's one human who's a clone for sure," said Prunella. "And that's Tom Hanks. No celebrity can be that nice."

"Oh, I think Tom Hanks really is that nice," I said.

Just then, a doctor came hurrying over, and all the humans got up from their plastic chairs.

"Family of Opal Harvey?" he asked.

"I'm her partner," said Harlan gravely.

"Your wife is in stable condition, Mr. Harvey. She will live."

"Oh, thank the Lord," said Harlan, raising his eyes heavenward.

"Was it the Botox, doctor?" asked Marilyn.

"Yes, it was. A severe allergic reaction. Her heart stopped for a moment, but we managed to bring her back."

"When can we see her?" asked Harlan.

"Not just yet. She's not fully awake. But I'll let you know as soon as she's in her room."

The doctor excused himself, and Harlan suddenly started crying.

"Why is he crying?" asked Dooley. "Isn't it good news that Opal will live?"

"Sometimes humans cry when they hear good news, too," I said.

"Weird," was Dooley's determination.

"They're happy tears," Harriet confirmed. "Look at his face. He's smiling."

"No, he's not," said Brutus. "The corners of his mouth are pointing down."

"He's happy, I'm telling you. Those are happy tears."

"Then why does he look sad?"

"Oh, Brutus."

And as my fellow cats argued back and forth about the tough task of interpreting human emotion, I tripped over to where Odelia had taken a seat again.

"Tough day, huh, Max?" she said.

"Yeah, tell me about it," I said. "I just found out I wasn't cloned, and I was so looking forward to meeting my original self, too."

She glanced over, and I gave her an exaggerated smile. "Irony. Very funny, Max."

"So what happened, exactly?"

"Well, apparently there was a mix-up at the salon and Opal, in spite of her strict instructions not to get Botox, got her second dose in a week, which almost proved lethal."

"But how could such a mix-up happen?"

Odelia looked over to Harlan, who was now being

comforted by Marilyn, and lowered her voice. "Someone phoned the salon, and said Opal wanted to have the full Botox treatment today. They were pretty adamant, too."

"They phoned the salon? But who?"

"All I know is that it was a woman's voice."

"A woman's voice. That must be our culprit."

"Opal really should get the police involved this time. They can track phones and find out where that call was coming from."

"If her assailant is clever they'll have used a burner phone," I pointed out.

"Yeah, I guess you're right. Still, the police have the kind of resources we don't."

"You'll figure it out," I said, having complete faith in my human. Well, except when I practically accused her of having me cloned and neglecting to tell me about it, of course.

"I'm not so sure, Max," she said, sounding and looking a little downhearted. "Opal almost got killed on my watch twice now. I think the moment she regains consciousness and hears about what happened, she's going to put us on the first flight home."

"No, she won't. She knows you're her best shot at catching whoever is behind this, and she's not going to lose faith in you just because—"

"I almost let her die twice?"

"We'll catch the person responsible," I said. "I just know we will."

She nodded, but I could tell she'd lost faith in herself. And I shouldn't wonder. She was right. Opal had almost died on her watch. People lost faith in themselves over less than that, especially when they'd been tasked not only with keeping their client alive but with catching the person trying to send them to an early grave—or the cloner's freezer.

I returned to my friends, thinking about this strange case.

It now appeared that a woman was behind this. How many women did we know who were involved with Opal and who had access to her home and the studio? Suzy, one of the members of her team, came to mind, and Helga, of course, though she seemed like a long shot. There were others, at least two dozen, who all worked side by side with Opal at the studio. Any one of them could be behind this. It was clear to me that Odelia had her work cut out for her.

"And?" said Prunella. "What's the latest?"

"Your human will live. The doctors anticipate a full recovery."

"Yay," said Prunella. "Though wouldn't it have been nice for her to be cloned, though? That way we could have been two clones together. Like clones in a pod."

I didn't know whether it was the cloning or if the original Prunella had a very peculiar sense of humor, too, but it did make me wonder about this whole cloning business. What if I went in a normal, regular Max and came out a fruitcake?

Food for thought.

27

Opal made a remarkable and downright miraculous recovery, and in spite of the doctor's insistence she stay in hospital overnight, she decided to discharge herself. A nurse had put her in a wheelchair and pushed her all the way to the exit before an indignant Opal got up before the collected paparazzi caught sight of her and then charged out of the hospital under her own steam, ignoring flashing lightbulbs and cameras until she'd reached her limo and had gotten in, slamming the door as she did.

The rest of the small company didn't garner the same attention Opal did, except for Marilyn. But she, too, ignored the barrage of questions hurled in her direction, and they all got into the second limo, which had pulled up right as Opal's limo had pulled out.

Soon they were on their way to a destination unknown, and the atmosphere in the limo was fraught with a mixture of elation and anxiousness. Elation that Opal had recovered so well, but also anxiousness that this could happen again, and that whoever was responsible was out there somewhere, plotting their next move.

"Opal needs to cancel her show," said Marilyn. "She needs to stay home until this person is caught."

"Yeah, and who is going to make her?" asked Harlan. "You? Me? Opal doesn't listen to anyone. You know that, Marilyn."

"We'll have to make her see reason, Harlan. She needs to be protected."

"She's not going to cancel her show, not now, not ever. She wouldn't cancel her show if someone dropped a bomb on her office. She's stubborn that way."

"It's amazing how quickly she recovered," said Marge. "A medical miracle."

"Not really," said Tex. "She suffered an extreme allergic reaction. People can come back from an episode like that very quickly."

"Thank God there was a doctor present," said Marge. "Who knows what would have happened otherwise."

Harlan grimaced. "I prefer not to let my mind go there, Mrs. Poole."

"Marge, please. And I completely understand."

"I'm just glad you had the presence of mind to call an ambulance, Odelia, and that they got there as quickly as they did."

"Does the salon have a recording of the person who called in?" asked Marilyn.

"No, unfortunately, they don't," said Odelia. "They just said the voice sounded young, though that doesn't mean anything, of course."

"A young woman," Marilyn said slowly as thought wrinkles appeared on her brow. "Maybe you should talk to Opal's staff again. Most of them are women."

"We're going into the studio tomorrow," said Odelia. "We'll talk to everyone."

"I thought there was no show on Sundays?" said Marge.

"There's no show on Sundays but the team starts preparing the Monday show on the Sunday," Marilyn explained. "Though Opal doesn't always join in. At this point it's a well-oiled machine, and she usually meets with her team on Monday morning."

"Where are we going, by the way?" asked Tex.

"The Villa Marguerite," said Harlan. "It's a great little restaurant in Sherman Oaks. We booked last week, and come hell or high water, Opal wasn't going to let that booking go to waste."

We arrived at the Villa Marguerite and got out. It was one of those ultra-fancy restaurants, and I was already licking my lips in anticipation of the feast we would be served.

Unfortunately soon after we arrived we cats were all relegated to the kitchen, as no pets were allowed in the dining room, and soon after we were all kicked out of the kitchen by an irate chef, and found ourselves in a back alley, which left a lot to be desired.

"Um… I was actually looking forward to having a sumptuous meal," said Prunella.

We stared at the row of dumpsters lining one wall, and a heap of rubble and garbage piled up against the other. It didn't look all that appetizing.

"Clarice would love this," said Brutus with profound affection.

"Who's Clarice?" asked Prunella.

"A friend of ours back home," I said. "She likes to eat in the rough."

"Oh, a feral cat?"

"Exactly, though she has mellowed out a little and has taken a liking to Odelia."

We took a seat on the wet cement floor behind the restaurant and even as I put my nose in the air and smelled all those delicious smells wafting from the vent attached to the kitchen, my stomach was grumbling louder and louder.

"Man, I'm hungry," said Brutus.

"Me, too," said Harriet sadly. Not only did she only have three paws whose nails had been buffed and polished, but now she had to place her perfectly white Persian tush on this dirty cement slab. A sad ending to a sad day.

Just then, two dogs came wandering up.

"Oh, God. Not dogs, too," Harriet lamented.

"Oh, hey, you guys," said the first dog, a male Schnauzer. "Any luck?"

"If you're referring to the food on offer, no luck, I'm afraid," I said.

"Hi, there," said the second dog, a lady Cocker Spaniel.

They both looked nice enough. I pegged them as a young couple.

"Tony is usually pretty punctual," said the lady.

"I guess we're early," said her mate, who looked like a tramp.

And as if he'd overheard the conversation, suddenly the backdoor to the restaurant swung open and a man came hurrying out. "Oh, have I got the feast for you tonight!" he said with a wide smile. He then plunked down a small table and placed a large dish of something that looked and smelled edible on top of it.

"Spaghetti and meatballs!" he cried, gesturing to the sizable pot. "Tuck in, my friends!"

We all got a little closer and he laughed. "Oh, I see you brought some friends tonight. Well, dig in. There's enough for everyone!"

"Gee, thanks, Tony," said the tramp, and took a seat at the table. Across from him, the lady dog also took a seat, and soon they were both putting their snouts into the big pot of pasta.

I looked at Dooley, Dooley looked at me. Harriet and Brutus shared a look. Prunella, though, didn't need encouragement. She was already digging in. "Come on, you guys," she said. "This stuff is delicious!"

I moved closer and took a bite. She was right. The stuff really was delicious.

Behind us, Tony stood watching. He clapped his hands and smiled. "You like?"

"Yeah, we like, Tony," said the lady dog.

"You did it again, Tony," said the tramp.

"I'm so happy!" Tony cried, and returned inside the kitchen.

"My name is Tramp, by the way," said the big dog, "and this here is Lady."

"Max," I said between two bites, and the others all introduced themselves as well.

It took me a while to make the connection, then I frowned and looked up at our two canine companions.

"Lady and the Tramp. You mean, like in the Disney movie?"

"Yeah, we're actors," said Tramp.

"That's us in the movie," Lady explained. "Well, our voices, anyway."

"But... that movie is... old."

Lady looked up and smiled sweetly at her mate. "The miracle of cloning, Max."

"Yeah, cloning is all the rage. We made our debut in 1955 and we've been going strong ever since. Isn't that right, sweetie-pie?"

"Absolutely, honey bunch."

"You hear that, Brutus? They sound exactly like us," said Harriet.

"They sure do, sugar plum," said Brutus, but he was too busy eating to say more.

"We did *Lady and the Tramp II*," said Lady.

"Straight to video," said Tramp.

"And then of course the live-action movie," said Lady. "We're very proud of that one."

"We're doing the sequel now," said Tramp.

"We make a pretty good living."

"Yeah, can't complain," said Tramp, and sucked in a string of pasta. As luck would have it, Lady was sucking in the same pasta string, only from the other side. When they met in the middle, they kissed—just like in the movie!

And as I picked out a meatball myself, I thought what a strange place this Hollywood was, and suddenly I was starting to feel homesick. This was a lot of fun, meeting stars like Lady and Tramp, but I was missing my friends. Kingman and Shanille and Clarice… They might not have been cloned or Botoxed or primped and tucked and pampered, but they were real. And they were my buddies.

Hampton Cove was suddenly starting to look really good.

28

Inside the restaurant, the atmosphere was downcast, which was hardly a surprise, as one of the members of the party had been discharged from hospital only hours before, and didn't exactly look hot to trot.

"You should go home," said Marilyn. "You look like death warmed up."

"Thanks for the compliment," said Opal.

"No, Marilyn is right," said her boyfriend. "You don't look so well, darling. Maybe we should call it a night. Get a good night's sleep."

"I'm not going to give whoever did this the satisfaction," said Opal stubbornly. "I was looking forward to tonight and I'm going to enjoy my meal and so are all of you. So shut up and eat."

Odelia thought Harlan and Marilyn were right. Opal's face was still swollen, especially her lips, which resembled those of a blowfish. It was hard to imagine how she managed to get down any of the food she was eating, considering the Botox allergy had closed up her throat and she clearly still had trouble swallowing.

"She looks terrible," Odelia's mother whispered. "Are you sure she's fine?"

"If she says she's fine, I guess she's fine," Odelia whispered back.

They were all sitting at a long table: Odelia and her family, Chase and Uncle Alec included, and Opal's party, which consisted of herself, Marilyn and Harlan. All in all, it was all very cozy, especially since they'd been given a table at the back by the maître d', where they wouldn't be bothered by other guests, and could enjoy their meal in private.

"She shouldn't have discharged herself," said Gran. "Mark my words—she'll be sorry."

"What do you think, Tex? You're the medical man," said Uncle Alec.

"I think nothing," said Dad as he devoted himself to his sirloin steak. "I'm here as a tourist, not a doctor."

"But shouldn't you say something? You did sign that oath of Pythagoras, didn't you?" Gran insisted.

"Hippocrates, and it's not my habit to go around dispensing medical advice just because I feel like it. Ultimately Opal is the custodian of her own health."

"Nice words, to hide the fact that you're too chicken to tell Opal what's what."

"I'm not too chicken to tell anyone anything, but Opal is a grown woman and she clearly knows what she's doing."

"A lot of baloney," Gran muttered, shaking her head.

"So how is the police conference going?" asked Odelia, eager to change the subject.

"Total bust," said Uncle Alec.

"Yeah, not at all what we expected," Chase chimed in.

"Some nonsense about using military tactics to police the community," said Alec. "Not on my watch. That's what I told that instructor and that's what I intend to tell the mayor."

"You didn't tell that instructor anything, and I'm pretty

sure you're not going to tell the mayor anything either," said Chase.

"Well, it's the thought that counts," said Uncle Alec vaguely. He'd ordered ribs and was enjoying them tremendously, judging from the sauce dripping from his chin.

"What did I tell you about eating lean meat only?" said Chase.

"This is lean meat only," said Uncle Alec.

"No, it's not. This is just about the greasiest stuff imaginable. Do you know what this is going to do to your arteries?"

"I don't know and I don't care. I'm enjoying my meal and if you could please focus on your own plate and not mine I'd be very much obliged, you fitness guru wannabe you."

"Your wellbeing is my concern, Alec," said Chase, who was starting to sound more and more like the chief's mother.

"Well, it shouldn't be."

Chase gave Odelia a comical grimace. "See what I'm dealing with here?"

"See what *I'm* dealing with?" said Alec.

Odelia patted her uncle on the arm. "Chase is right, Uncle Alec. And he's only saying this because he cares. If you keep eating like this you'll get yourself in trouble."

"No, I won't. Tell them, Tex. Tell them I'm as healthy as an ox."

"You know I can't divulge confidential information about my patients, Alec," said Dad, slicing into his steak with the precision of a brain surgeon.

"But I'm telling you to tell them. I'm absolving you of your doctor-patient privilege."

"Still, I feel reluctant to share that kind of information with a third party."

"She's my niece, for God's sakes!"

"Fine. Alec, you are a heart attack waiting to happen. It wouldn't surprise me if one of these days you're going to need triple bypass surgery—possibly quadruple. There. That enough information for you?"

Alec stared at his brother-in-law in horror. "You never told me that."

"I told you exactly that," said Dad. "Trouble is you never listen."

"Quadruple bypass surgery?"

"Look on the bright side. Could have been quintuple," said Dad with faux cheer.

Alec had placed the uneaten rib back on his plate and slowly lifted his napkin to his lips. "Thanks, Doc," he said with a wounded expression on his face. "Thanks for ruining a perfectly good dinner."

"You're welcome," said Dad with the kind of smile he reserved for patients on the brink of death, to calm them down while the ambulance was on its way.

"Looks like I'm not the only one facing health issues," said Opal.

"I'm not facing any health issues," said Alec. "I'm pretty sure my brother-in-law is just kidding. Isn't that right, Tex? You're just kidding, right?"

"I'm a doctor," said Dad. "I never kid about bypass surgery."

"It's all those burgers," said Marge. "I told my husband we should stop organizing backyard barbecues. All that fat and all of that meat is clogging up my poor brother's arteries, and soon he'll be dead and where will that leave us?"

"With Chase as the new chief of police, probably," said Dad, stoically slicing and dicing his steak. Odelia had to admire her father's capacity to focus. Probably something that came with the job.

"See?" said Chase. "What did I tell you, buddy? If you don't adopt a healthier lifestyle Hampton Cove will lose a great chief, and then the mayor will make me chief and the system will break down. I'm not cut out to be chief. I'm a detective, not an administrator. So please take better care of yourself and save me from being the new chief."

The Chief was frowning at his deputy. "Nice speech. But who says the mayor will make you the new chief? I'll bet he'll appoint his niece instead. And then you'll be taking orders from her."

"All the more reason for you to lose the flab and stay chief forever," said Chase, patting Uncle Alec's protruding belly.

Alec grunted something under his breath and shoved his plate away.

"Aren't you going to eat those?" asked Harlan.

"I guess not," said Uncle Alec, his face a mask of pretty petulance.

"Can I have a stab?" asked Harlan.

"Oh, Harlan," said his partner of thirty years.

"Go ahead," said Alec, and handed Harlan his plate.

"Thanks," said Harlan. "I love spare ribs."

"Me, too," said the Chief mournfully. He'd brought a hand to his chest, and was presumably thinking about Dad's words. A quadruple bypass was not a pleasant prospect, and it appeared that Odelia's dad's words had touched a chord.

"I've told you before and I'll tell you again," said Marge. "You should listen to Tex. Tex knows."

"Yeah, yeah, yeah," said Uncle Alec.

"Is it true that you're a doctor, Mr. Poole?" asked Marilyn now.

"Tex, please," said Dad with an engaging smile. He might be able to conjure up absolute focus when dealing with his sirloin steak, but even he was susceptible to the charms of a famous talk show host like Marilyn Coyn.

"I have a mole on my thigh," said Marilyn. "My doctor tells me it's nothing to worry about, but I would love to get a second opinion. Can you take a look?"

And before awaiting Dad's response, she was already hiking up her dress and shoving her thighs in the good doctor's face.

Dad, redirecting his attention from his steak to Marilyn's thighs, didn't even flinch. As a doctor he was used to random strangers walking up to him on the street and showing them their spots. He studied Marilyn's mole, which was, Odelia saw, a nice purple one.

"Nothing to worry about," said Dad, showcasing his suavest bedside manner. "Absolutely harmless, Mrs. Coyn."

"You really think so, doctor?" asked Marilyn, a note of concern in her voice. "When I scratch it my left ear tickles."

"Perfectly harmless little mole."

"I'm worried it might be cancer."

"Well, I can assure you that it's not."

"Do you think I should have it removed?"

"That's entirely up to you, my dear Mrs. Coyn," he said smoothly. "If the mole bothers you so much, by all means have it removed. If not, it can't hurt to leave it untouched."

"Thank you so much, doctor," she said, almost purring now.

Odelia caught her mother's eye, and saw she wasn't impressed with Marilyn's attempts to snag her husband's attention. Then again, as the wife of the only doctor in town, Marge had had to endure quite a lot over the years. Women practically throwing themselves at her husband's feet, grown men dropping their pants in the middle of the street and bending over… It took more than a Hollywood star shoving her crotch in Dad's face to phase her and she clearly wasn't phased now.

"Speaking of moles," said Harlan, clearing his throat. "I have a strange growth on my buttocks. Can I bother you to take a gander, Doctor Poole?"

And so instead of finishing his steak, Tex dutifully examined first the hairy wart on Harlan's hairy buttocks, then a mole shaped like a cauliflower on Opal's chest, and finally yet another odd-looking mole on one of the waitstaff's feet. When finally the restaurant's owner dropped by and dropped his pants, Odelia decided to excuse herself and go in search of her cats. All these moles and warts had seriously caused her to lose her appetite, and when she emerged through the kitchen and out the backdoor, she was surprised to find her cats fraternizing with two dogs, all of them seated around a big bowl of what must have been spaghetti, as only a few remnants of the stuff were left in the pot. They were all chatting amicably, and clearly having a great time.

"Oh, hey, Odelia," said Harriet. "Meet the real Lady and the Tramp. They're actors."

Odelia greeted the two dogs, and even though she couldn't understand what they were saying—she could understand feline but not canine—it was obvious they were in great spirits.

"Pull up a chair," said Brutus. "Tony's food is seriously out of this world."

So she pulled up a chair, and when Tony emerged from the kitchen, carrying a big vanilla cake, he didn't even look surprised to find that he was now serving his best dishes to a mixed feline, canine and human company.

And as she sampled the most delicious vanilla cake she'd ever tasted, she thought not for the first time that sometimes she felt more comfortable in the company of her pets than in that of other humans. Then again, was that so strange? She was, after all, a cat lady, through and through, as Chase had so often told her.

Moments later, Chase came ambling out to get some fresh air, and at Odelia's instigation took a seat, too. And when finally Uncle Alec, Marge and Gran followed suit, the Poole family was complete. Only Tex was missing, but then he was probably busy studying more moles that had mysteriously appeared on a Hollywoodian thigh or butt.

"It's nice out here," said Marge.

"It is," Gran agreed. "Very nice."

"Have you found Hank yet?" asked Odelia.

"No, not yet. I hope nothing happened to him."

"I'm sure he'll be fine," said Marge.

Gran didn't seem convinced.

"So what happens now?" asked Max.

"Well, now we talk to the members of Opal's staff," said Odelia. "Only Opal gave us strict instructions not to divulge anything about what happened today, so we're a little handicapped."

"But we came up with a plan," said Gran. "A very clever plan, if I say so myself."

"Well? What's the plan?" asked Harriet.

"We'll let all of the ladies record a message and then we'll play that message to the girl from the spa who picked up the phone. She's assured us she would recognize that voice out of a thousand." She beamed at her present company.

Lady said something that Odelia didn't understand, so Max translated. "Lady says it sounds like a great plan, and she hopes you'll catch whoever is responsible. She's a big fan of Opal and wouldn't want anything to happen to her."

"Thanks, Lady," said Odelia.

It was the best plan they'd been able to come up with. Odelia had actually suggested to bring Uncle Alec and Chase in. They were both experienced cops and would be able to help them conduct the interviews. But Opal had put her foot down once more: no cops, and no one was to find out what was going on.

Tough to catch a killer with not one but two hands tied behind your back, though.

29

The next day saw a long procession of Opal's staff members file in and out of the meeting room. Opal had told them she was working on some ideas for a new segment, and she wanted their voices on tape so she could pick one to do the voice-over for the new bit. None of them seemed suspicious about the ruse. On the contrary, they were all excited to read the two lines: 'Hi, this is Opal Harvey's personal assistant. Just touching base to let you know that Mrs. Harvey will be having the full Botox treatment this morning. Yes, that's right. The full Botox treatment. Lips, brow, chest and cheeks.'

I didn't think they'd fall for the ruse but they had—happily! Of course, the substantial bonus Opal had promised probably had something to do with their enthusiasm.

"Did I get the part?" asked Suzy excitedly, her pigtails bouncing and her glasses sliding from her nose. "You can tell me, I won't tell the others."

"How long have you worked for Opal, Suzy?" asked Gran.

"Um, going on five years now, I think. A long time, huh? I

never thought I'd last this long. Opal has a reputation for hiring and firing quicker than her shadow, so..."

"But you stuck it out. And why do you think that is?" asked Odelia, following her grandmother's cue.

"Oh, I don't know. I guess I'm more eager than most to make this work. I don't want to stay in this position forever, you know. I want to reach the top myself, if I can."

"You mean... host your own show one day?"

The plump young woman nodded eagerly. "That's the plan. Only there aren't that many opportunities out there for potential show hosts. So you have to grab what you can and show the bosses that you're willing to do whatever it takes to move up the ranks."

"Make sure they notice you," said Gran.

"Exactly! Which is why I joined Opal's team."

"More opportunities here than in other places."

"Oh, definitely. Opal is a tough taskmaster, but she's also the best of the best. If you can make it here, you can make it anywhere, as the song goes."

"One more question," said Gran. "Do you know something about brake lines?"

After Suzy had left, Odelia discussed the interviews with her grandmother. "I think it's that Suzy," said the old lady. "She's clearly an ambitious little hustler, and prepared to do whatever it takes to reach the top. She probably figured if she could bump off Opal, the network bosses would hand her the show on a silver platter."

"Let's wait and see what the results of the recordings are," said Odelia, "before jumping to conclusions." She'd already sent the audio files to the beauty salon, and they were eagerly awaiting the verdict. It would probably take a little while, as the girl had to listen to all the recordings.

Finally, after a very tense twenty minutes, Odelia's phone dinged. She picked up and put it on speaker.

"Hey there, Janice," she said. "Did you get a chance to listen to the recordings?"

"I did, yeah," said the young woman.

"And?" asked Gran. "Who was it?"

"Well, I listened twice, as I didn't want to make a mistake, and I think it's audio file number fourteen."

"Audio file number fourteen," said Odelia, checking her list. And as her finger slid down the page, it finally landed on… Suzy.

"See?!" said Gran triumphantly. "I told you it was her!"

"Are you quite sure, Janice?" asked Odelia.

"Yeah, pretty sure. Of course, I didn't really pay attention yesterday, and a lot of these voices sound the same, but one thing really struck me."

"What's that?"

"The person on the phone sounded nice. I mean, not all voices sound nice, you know, but this one did. I remember thinking, this person is so nice and professional. And only recording fourteen had that quality. That upbeat quality, if you know what I mean."

Gran shook her head, indicating she had no idea what the girl was talking about, but Odelia said, "I know exactly what you mean, Janice. Thank you so much. You've been a tremendous help."

"Glad I could help. Will Opal be all right? We all feel terrible about what happened."

"She's fine."

And she was. That morning, Opal's lips and face had been back to their natural proportions, and the swelling in her throat had completely disappeared, too.

Odelia rang off and shared a grim look with her grandmother. "So now what?"

"Now we tell Opal and she'll have to take care of the tricky part."

"Call the police, you mean, and have Suzy arrested."

"Exactly. Our work here is done, honey." And she raised her hand for a high five, which Odelia half-heartedly slapped.

"What? You don't look happy."

"It's just that… the evidence is a little thin, don't you think? All we have to go on are the words of Janice, and she wasn't even a hundred percent sure."

"Good enough for me! You heard Suzy. She's one ambitious young lady, and can't wait to rise up in the world of showbiz. The only person standing in her way is Opal, so she decided to move things along by bumping her off. Easy peasy. Come on. Let's get out of here. I'm sick and tired of this Opal business."

"And here I thought you were her biggest fan."

"*Was* her biggest fan."

They walked out of the conference room and into Opal's office. Contrary to her custom, Opal had come in to work on a Sunday, as eager as Odelia and Vesta to find out who the culprit was.

"And? How did it go?" asked Opal as she rose from behind her desk. On top of her desk Prunella was softly snoring. Odelia's own cats were in the studio canteen, enjoying a meal. Odelia hadn't wanted to bring them in today, not seeing the point of dragging them out there again while they could simply stay at the house and enjoy its surrounding gardens and Helga's cooking, but the foursome had insisted they join her. They hadn't sat in on the interviews, as that would have been a little hard to explain.

"We got her," said Gran triumphantly.

"Who was it?" asked Opal anxiously.

"Suzy Parker," said Odelia. "Janice formally recognized her voice."

"Suzy!" said Opal, and dropped back down in her

ergonomic chair. "Oh, sweet Jesus. She's the best one I've got."

"Well, she did it," said Gran. "Do you want me to get her in here? You can interrogate her yourself. I'm sure she'll confess immediately."

"Yeah. Yeah, that might not be such a bad idea. Anything to keep this out of the press." She shook her head as Gran hurried out. "I don't believe this. Suzy. I trained her myself. I thought one day she'd take over from me. She's got it, you know, whatever it is. Bright, charismatic, beautiful, and she genuinely likes the job."

"You were grooming her to take over?"

"Yeah, well, not officially, but she's best suited for the job."

The door opened and Gran walked in with Suzy, who sported a smile from ear to ear.

Opal cleared her throat and sat up a little straighter. "Suzy. Take a seat, please."

"Did I get the job?" asked the girl, who was, indeed, very vivacious, Odelia thought.

"Well… see the thing is…"

"You've been caught red-handed, my dear," said Gran, who didn't believe in beating about the bush.

"Red-handed?" asked Suzy, turning to Gran. "What do you mean?"

"Let me handle this, Vesta," said Opal. "Look, Suzy. There's no easy way to say this, but—"

"You thought you could get away with it, didn't you?" said Gran. "Couldn't wait for Opal to retire so you decided to speed things up a little. Bump her off. Well, you were careless, young lady."

"Vesta," said Opal. "I'll handle this, all right? Suzy, I'd hate to call the police and have you arrested, so if you come clean now, maybe there's a way we can deal with this without involving the law. But you have to tell me everything."

"I don't understand," said Suzy, her eyes playing ping-pong between Odelia, Gran and Opal. "What's all this about bumping you off?"

"First you cut her brake lines, then you poisoned her coffee, then you dumped a light fixture on her head, and yesterday you tried to have her killed by Botox overdose!" said Gran, pointing an accusatory finger in the young woman's face. "Confess, you murderous vixen! Confess!"

"Vesta!"

"I don't—brake lines? Poisoned coffee? I have no idea what you're talking about!" said Suzy, her smile having vanished and been replaced with a look of utter confusion.

Either she was a very good actress, Odelia thought, or she really had no idea what was going on.

"You tried to kill me, Suzy," said Opal. "Several times. Why?"

"Yes, why did you do it—confess!" Gran cried.

"I didn't do it!" said Suzy. "I didn't try to kill you. I never came near your car, I never poisoned any coffee, and I have no idea what you mean with death by Botox!"

"Oh, bullshit," said Gran, and gestured to Odelia. "Play the recording, Odelia. Play it!"

And Odelia played it.

"That's me," said Suzy. "That's my audition tape."

"Your voice was formally recognized as belonging to the woman who phoned my beauty salon yesterday," said Opal, "instructing them to administer a Botox dose that could have been fatal."

"You phoned the salon!" said Gran. "You did that! Not smart, young lady! Not smart at all!"

"But I never called anyone! Whoever called the salon, it wasn't me."

"Suzy Parker," said Opal in her best authoritative voice.

"If you don't confess now, there's nothing more I can do for you. I'll have to hand this matter to the police."

"But I promise you, Opal," said Suzy, on the verge of tears now. "It wasn't me!"

"Oh, playing coy now, are we?" said Gran. "You weren't so coy when you dumped that cyanide into Opal's coffee, were you?"

"I never came near Opal's coffee!"

"That's probably true," said Opal with a frown. "I was poisoned at the house, and Suzy has only been at the house once, to deliver some documents."

"She could have snuck in," said Gran. "Not hard to do. Not hard at all."

"Unlikely," said Opal, shaking her head. "I have pretty good security. If she'd tried to sneak in, she would have been caught."

"See!" said Suzy. "I didn't do it, Opal. I swear to God!"

"Okay, fine," said Opal. "I believe you. But then who did?"

"I don't know. Honestly, I don't."

"You're not going to let her off the hook that easily, are you?" asked Gran, sounding disappointed. "She did it!"

Opal seemed to be of two minds about Suzy, and to be fair, Odelia couldn't blame her. It was hard to see in Suzy a hardened killer. Frankly she didn't think she did it, either.

"Haven't you noticed anything out of the ordinary lately?" asked Opal. "Someone saying something weird, acting suspicious?"

Suzy was shaking her head. "Nothing. We all love you here, Opal. We adore you. We wouldn't do anything to harm you. None of us."

"Well, someone did," said Opal, "and if it wasn't you, it was one of your colleagues."

"I vouch for them," said Suzy, lifting her chin. "I vouch for each and every one of them."

"Oh, hell," said Opal, leaning back. "This is a nightmare."

Just then, her phone sang out a tune, and she picked it up. She listened for a moment, then her eyes widened and she put the phone on speaker. "Can you say that again?" she asked in a shaky voice.

"I said, I have your friend Marilyn," a metallic voice spoke. "And if you want to see her alive again, you will come to Bluff Point at midnight, with a million dollars in cash. Alone. No cops."

"But… I don't have that kind of money!"

The metallic voice broke into a menacing laugh. "Yeah, right. Billionaire Opal Harvey doesn't have a million dollars. That's chump change for you, lady. I suggest you do as you're told, or else I'll mail you back your friend in pieces, starting with her fingers!"

"No, wait!" Opal cried, but the line had already gone dead.

30

We were all back at the house. Once again Opal had ignored Odelia's urgent advice to call in the police, but at least this time she'd allowed her to call in the help of Chase and Uncle Alec.

Opal was pacing the floor of her study while Odelia and Gran, Marge and Tex, Chase and Uncle Alec, and of course Harlan sat around, biting their nails as the hours crept by.

At midnight Opal was to deliver the sum of money to the kidnapper, and even though she'd told the man she wouldn't be able to raise the money, she had managed anyway.

"Tough to raise a million dollars on a Sunday," Brutus said now.

We were, as usual, on the sidelines while the humans talked back and forth about the terrible ordeal Marilyn Coyn must be going through. This time we weren't ensconced beneath the desk, but had managed to secure ourselves a position on the windowsill. A real window seat it was, too, and very comfortably outfitted with very soft cushions.

"Opal always keeps cash in the house," Prunella said. "She likes the security of knowing her money is close."

"Doesn't she trust banks?" I asked.

"No, she doesn't. Ever since a couple of banks collapsed some years ago, she keeps a big chunk of her money in her safe."

"Must be a big safe," said Brutus, "to keep all those billions."

"She's not a billionaire, silly," said Prunella.

"She's not? But I thought—"

"That's just more media nonsense. They print a lot of lies about Opal. She's a millionaire a couple of times over, but hardly a billionaire."

"So where does she keep her money?"

Prunella pointed to a painting of Opal that was suspended on the wall behind her desk. "It swings open," she said. "Behind it is her safe, where she keeps stacks of cash, jewelry, gold bars, and cigars."

"Cigars? You mean, like, gold cigars?"

"No, real cigars. They're Harlan's, and he's always afraid someone will steal them."

"Rich people," Brutus muttered.

"She shouldn't go out there all by herself," said Harriet. "It's not safe."

"No, that guy has tried to kill her three times already," I said. "He won't hesitate to try again."

"Guy? I thought Opal's assailant was a woman?" asked Brutus.

"I thought so, too, but Odelia said the voice on the phone sounded male."

"He probably changed his voice when he called the salon yesterday," Brutus said.

"Or maybe she altered her voice when she called Opal today," said Harriet.

Both were distinct possibilities, and it was hard to know which one was correct.

"So what's the plan?" asked Brutus.

"Opal will drive out there alone, to deliver the money," I said.

"But she won't be alone, will she?" said Prunella. "I—we'll all be in the car with her. And if something happens, we'll pounce on the assailant and rip him—"

"Or her," I interjected.

"—to shreds."

"Sounds like a plan," Brutus agreed.

"And of course Odelia and the others will all be close by, keeping their distance so as not to spook the kidnapper, but close enough so that they can get there in seconds."

"Minutes," I corrected her.

"Minutes isn't good enough," said Brutus. "It only takes a second to fire a fatal shot."

"Oh, dear," said Prunella. "I knew she should have had those cloning people take a sample of her living tissue."

The night crept on, with the clock seemingly ticking slower as midnight drew near.

"Oh, this is horrible!" Opal exclaimed as she traced a pattern on her nice Oriental rug. "This waiting around—it's enough to drive me crazy!"

"That's probably the idea," said her boyfriend. "It's a form of psychological warfare. They know this is driving you crazy, and that's exactly what they want."

"At least now we know for sure it isn't Suzy doing this," said Opal.

"Unless she's working in cahoots with a second party," said Gran, who still hadn't given up on Suzy as the mastermind behind all of this.

"I think we can safely exclude Suzy from our list of suspects," said Odelia.

The door opened and the hundred-year-old butler shuffled in. He was carrying a tray with a teapot, cups and saucers, and biscuits. "Tea and cookies, ma'am," he announced in a reedy voice.

His hands were shaking, and I was nine-ninety percent sure he'd soon drop the entire tray on the floor. Much to my surprise, though, he kept on shuffling until he'd reached a little gate-leg table and managed to deposit the tray on top of it unscathed.

"Thank you, Barkley," said Opal.

"Will there be anything else, ma'am?" asked the ancient retainer.

"No, you go to bed now."

"Thank you, ma'am—sir." And he shuffled out again, closing the door as he went.

"We never thought to put him on our list of suspects," said Gran, annoyed at this oversight on her part.

"Barkley? He's been with us for years," said Harlan.

"Yeah, Barkley wouldn't do such a thing," said Opal.

"I think we can exclude the centenarian," was Chase's opinion. "You really don't want me to hide in the backseat of the car, Opal?" he asked, reiterating an idea he'd launched earlier in the evening.

"No, if the kidnapper sees even a glimpse of you, they're likely to open fire."

"I could hide in the trunk," Chase amended his original plan.

"And what good would that do? By the time you're out of that trunk, the transaction will have either been concluded, or gone horribly awry. No, I have to do this myself. This is my mess. I put Marilyn in this position and I have to get her out."

"I hope she'll be all right," said Marge, who was clutching her neck.

"If that bastard has harmed even a single hair on the poor woman's head," Harlan began, reddening beneath his tan, "I'll... I'll... Well, I don't know what I'll do but I'll do something!"

"I know you will, darling," said Opal, pressing her boyfriend's hand. "I know. But we need to stay positive here. We need to think good thoughts and hope for the best."

Soon it was time to leave, and Opal grabbed hold of the bulky bag with cash and walked out, followed by a procession of well-wishers and fellow positive thinkers. Except for Gran, who probably never read a positive thinking book in her life.

"We're all gonna die," she said now, earning herself a scowl from Opal.

We followed them into the hallway and then outside, where four cars were parked.

For the occasion Opal had decided not to use the limo—or her driver—but to use a less conspicuous mode of transportation instead. She was going to drive a bright red Mini Cooper, Harlan got behind the wheels of one of his Ferraris, while Odelia had been granted the rare privilege of selecting a car from Harlan's extensive collection. She'd opted for a nice Fiat 500, with Gran riding shotgun, and Marge and Tex squeezing into the backseat. Alec and Chase, finally, were in the rental Toyota they'd gotten at the Grand Continental.

We cats all filed into Opal's Mini Cooper, and then the fleet drove out of the gates and set a course for Bluff Point, where Marilyn's fate would soon be decided.<>

31

"It's a real pity your human doesn't speak our language," I said, "or else we could have given her some instructions."

"What instructions? She knows how to spend money," said Prunella. "Even a million."

"Not about spending the money," I said, "but how to deal with this kidnapper."

"And what would you advise her? To attack him and make sure she doesn't get shot?"

"Not exactly. I'd advise her to stay calm and under no circumstances to provoke him."

"Or her," said Harriet, still adamant that Opal's assailant was a woman.

"Why do you insist the kidnapper is a guy, Max?" asked Brutus.

"I told you. Odelia said the voice of the kidnapper sounded like a male voice."

"Plus, only men do stupid things like try to kill a person or kidnap their best friend," said Prunella.

"No, they don't. There are plenty of women killers," said

Harriet, who apparently had very pronounced views on the matter.

"Just look at the statistics, Harriet," said Prunella. "Ninety percent of the people convicted of homicide are men. Very few lady killers out there."

"Plenty of ladykillers, though," Brutus muttered.

"Well, I think you're wrong," said Harriet stubbornly. "Women can do crime just as well as men, and to think otherwise suggests a world view that's outdated and, frankly, bigoted, Prunella. Anything men do, women can do better—even crime. So there."

"They can, but they don't, because as a rule women are much smarter than men."

"No, they're not!" said Harriet, then gulped.

"Ha! Gotcha!" said Prunella, and laughed loudly.

"Oh, my darlings," said Opal, holding on to the steering wheel with an iron grip. "I know you're scared, but please don't be. This will all be over soon."

"She thinks we're scared," said Dooley. "Why is that, Max?"

"Because she can't make the distinction between cats arguing and cats yowling in anguish," I said.

"Look, just hide in the back," said Opal. "From the moment we arrive, just stay low and don't show yourselves. I'm not going to give this bad person an excuse to shoot you."

Just then, her phone sang out Chickie Hay's biggest hit. 'Wake me up,' Chickie sang, and Opal woke up her phone by pressing the Connect button.

"Phoning and driving is very dangerous," said Dooley.

"Shush, Dooley," said Harriet. "It's probably the kidnapper."

"Yes, this is Opal?" She'd put the phone on speaker, so she could keep both hands on the wheel.

"Very sensible," said Dooley.

"Shush already, will you?" said Harriet.

"Did you do as you were told?" the same metallic voice sounded over the phone.

"Yes, I did. I'm all alone in the car," she said, darting a cautious look in her rearview mirror at the five of us. "And I've got the money."

"Good." And he—or she—promptly disconnected again.

"It's not far now," said Opal. "We're almost there."

She was right. Within seconds she slowed down the car, and when I took a peek through the window I saw we'd arrived at what looked like the surface of the moon: only rocks were visible, and it was very dark out, with a sliver of moon lending some measure of illumination.

"Looks pretty creepy out there," I remarked.

"Keep your head down, Max!" said Brutus. "You don't want to get shot, do you?"

"No, I don't," I admitted, and retracted my head.

Opal stopped the car and got out, dragging her bulky bag full of cash along with her.

I couldn't resist the temptation so I stuck my head up again. What good was it to tag along like this if we couldn't help Opal and try to identify this horrible person?

She'd left the car door open, so I snuck out.

"Max!" said Harriet. "What are you doing?"

"Taking a closer look!" I hissed.

Behind me, Dooley followed in my wake, and so did Prunella and then, finally, Harriet and Brutus.

A car stood parked about fifty yards from Opal's, its beams turned up high. It was hard to make out the figure standing next to the car, but as we made a circular movement and approached him or her, I could see that there were actually two figures. Moving even closer, I saw that one was Marilyn and the other was…

"Is that a man or a woman?" asked Dooley.

"I don't know. He or she is wearing a mask," I said.

They were also dressed in black from head to toe, and holding something that looked like a gun.

"Drop the bag!" the kidnapper shouted.

Opal did as she was told and dropped the bag. She then stood there for a moment, caught in the car's high beams.

"Where is Marilyn?" she yelled. "You promised to let her go if I paid you the money!"

"Step back!" said the kidnapper. "Back to your car. Now!"

"Not without Marilyn!" said Opal bravely.

The kidnapper pushed Marilyn and she stumbled into the beam of light.

"Marilyn!" Opal cried.

"I'm all right!" said Marilyn.

"Start walking," the kidnapper growled, and Marilyn started walking. When she and the kidnapper had reached the bag, he said, "Open the bag. Do it!"

Marilyn opened the bag and the kidnapper peered inside.

"We should attack," said Prunella. "Jump them and dig our claws in."

"And risk Marilyn getting hurt?" I said. "No way. We have to wait until she's safe."

The kidnapper appeared satisfied with the contents of the bag, for they now picked it up and started back for the car.

Marilyn, who just stood there for a moment, finally realized she was free and started running in the direction of her friend.

Suddenly a shot rang out, and Opal uttered a bloodcurdling scream.

"He shot her!" Brutus said.

"She shot her!" Harriet cried.

"Attack!" Dooley yelled, and without delay ran in the direction of the kidnapper.

We all followed suit, but unfortunately by the time we

reached the car, the dastardly devil had already stepped inside and slammed the door.

We watched helplessly as the car's tires spun, kicking up a cloud of dust and dirt, and soon the car was hurtling away at a high rate of speed.

"Opal!" said Prunella, and once again we were on the move, racing for Prunella's human this time. When we reached her we saw it was bad. She was covered in blood, lying on the ground, with Marilyn hovering over her, screaming her head off.

32

By the time Odelia reached Opal and Marilyn, the kidnapper was long gone, with the bag of money.

"Call an ambulance," said Tex as he knelt down next to the fallen talk show host. After a quick examination, which Odelia's dad carried out with practiced ease, he nodded. "It's just a flesh wound," he said, much to Odelia's relief. "The bullet hit her shoulder and went straight through. He was probably aiming for her heart, but missed."

"Oh, thank God," said Marilyn.

Opal opened her eyes and groaned. "Not again," were the first words out of her mouth. She looked up at Tex, and asked, "Am I going to live, doc?"

"Yes, Opal," he said with a reassuring smile. "You're going to be just fine. Though you will be sore for a while, and the wound needs to be cleaned and dressed."

"Oh, darling," said Harlan as he practically pounced on his girlfriend and took her into his arms.

She winced. "Careful, darling."

Harlan hugged her close, not caring that her blood got

onto his clothes, and Tex got up again. In the distance, the sound of an ambulance could already be heard.

Odelia's cats came walking up.

"How is she?" asked Prunella anxiously.

"She'll live," said Max, who'd overheard Dad's words.

"Oh, man," said Prunella. "Why did I have to pick a human who keeps almost dying on me! It's so stressful!"

Harriet, Brutus and Dooley laughed at this, but Max looked serious.

"We couldn't see his face," he said.

"Her face, you mean," said Harriet.

"I thought it was a man's voice," said Brutus.

"And I thought it sounded like a woman," said Harriet.

"Did you recognize him or her?" asked Odelia anxiously.

But Max shook his head. "No, I'm sorry. They were wearing a mask."

"The car was a dark blue town car," said Brutus, "though it could have been dark brown, dark green or dark red, and it could have been a sedan, I'm not entirely sure."

"So did they catch him?" asked Gran, who came hurrying up, panting heavily.

"No, they didn't. He managed to get away before they got close," said Odelia.

"Oh, darn it," said Gran. "I'll bet it was that Suzy woman though. She had homicidal maniac written all over her face."

"This vacation is really turning into a Hollywood movie," said Marge, who stood hugging herself. It was chilly out there, and she hadn't brought a coat. Chase, always the gentleman, must have noticed, too, for he took off his jacket and draped it around Marge's shoulders.

"Thanks, honey," said Marge gratefully.

"So the kidnapper got away?" asked Uncle Alec.

"Yeah, got away clean," said Chase.

"Took the money?"

"Took the money and fired off a shot—which hit Opal in the shoulder."

"Man, if this were Hampton Cove we'd be organizing a manhunt now."

Odelia walked up to Opal. "Are you still sure about not involving the police?"

"No police," Opal croaked. "The important thing is we have Marilyn back."

"He tried to kill you!" said Marilyn. "You have to go to the police, Opal."

"No police!" Opal insisted with a grimace of pain. "If the media finds out it's going to be a feeding frenzy." She turned to her friend. "Did you get a good look at the guy?"

"I'm not even sure it was a guy," said Marilyn. "Could have been a woman. He or she never took off their mask."

"How did it happen?" asked Chase. "How did they get you?"

"I'd just arrived home after our night out, and I'd just put my car in the garage when I was attacked from behind. They pushed some rag into my face and the next thing I knew I woke up in the backseat of that car, with a terrible headache and feeling nauseous."

"Chloroform," said Uncle Alec, nodding. "And then what happened?"

"And then we were driving and he parked the car and waited for you to arrive."

"He didn't talk to you?" asked Chase.

"Not a word. I demanded to know what he intended to do with me but nothing. Like talking to a wall. My hands were tied, and the doors locked, so I couldn't escape."

"What about the phone call? Did he say anything?"

"They got out to make that call. I couldn't hear a thing." She pressed her eyes closed and shivered. "It was horrible. The absolute most terrifying moments of my entire life."

"It's over now," said Harlan, placing an arm around her shoulder. "It's all over now."

"I'll never feel safe again."

"You need to hire security," said Chase.

"I know. And I will. Though I hate to go through life looking over my shoulder all the time." She turned to Odelia. "Do you have any idea who's doing this? Any idea at all?"

Odelia was embarrassed by her response. "Not a clue, to be honest."

"Oh, we do have a clue," said Gran. "It's that Suzy woman, I'm a hundred percent sure."

"No, it's not," said Odelia. "Suzy was with us when the kidnapper called."

"So? She could have had an accomplice. A boyfriend or whatever."

"Oh, Gran," said Odelia.

"What?! It's a plausible theory. We need to give her the first degree. Go good cop bad cop on her. Alec, you tell her. You know how it works."

"I'm usually the good cop," said Alec.

"No, you're not," said Chase. "I'm the good cop, and you're the bad cop."

"Let's not split hairs," Alec grumbled.

"Can't you interview her?" asked Opal.

"We don't have jurisdiction here," said Alec. "Not as good cops, or bad cops. We're civilians, just like you. With no rights to arrest people, or to subject them to questioning."

"It wasn't Suzy," said Opal. "That much I know." She sighed deeply. "But then who was it?"

33

You would have thought that Opal, after yet another trip to the emergency room, would finally have decided to chuck it in and take a nice long vacation, but no. The next day she insisted on heading into the studio to do her Monday show.

"But *I* can do your show," Marilyn had said. "I can easily take over for a couple of days—weeks, even."

"No, thanks," Opal had said. "It's my show and I'm going to be there to run it. Bullets fired at me or not. It's you who should rest, darling. You were the one being kidnapped."

So the next day we were all back at the studio. Or at least Odelia and Gran were, and their entire cat contingent, of course.

Tex and Marge had gone into town again, this time to Universal Studios to get the studio tour, and Chase and Uncle Alec had their conference to attend. Apparently the mayor had gotten wind that they'd been skipping lectures and had called Uncle Alec to give him a piece of his mind. It hadn't been pretty.

Opal and her team were holed up inside the conference

room, discussing that afternoon's show, and even Suzy was present, even though she could have been excused for staying home—or handing in her resignation.

"Max?" asked Dooley as we lounged around in Opal's office, interspersed with long visits to the canteen, where our food bowls were located.

"Yes, Dooley?"

"What is a toodle pip?"

"Toodle pip is not a thing but a greeting," I said. "And if I'm not mistaken it's something the Brits like to say. Basically it means goodbye."

He was silent for a moment while he chewed on this. Then he said, "So is Kurtz a Brit?"

"Not that I know, why?"

"Well, he said toodle pip when he dropped by the house for his interview with Odelia."

"I'm sure he just said it as a joke," I said. "I don't think he's British."

"And then there's the kidnapper," said Dooley. "He said the same thing last night."

I stared at my friend.

"What is he saying, Max?" asked Brutus.

"Wait, let me get this straight," I said. "You heard the kidnapper say toodle pip?"

"Yeah, when we were running to the car. I got there first, remember? And just before he slammed the door, he looked at me and said 'toodle pip.' Which I thought was odd."

"Well, I'll be damned," I said.

"What did he say, Max?" asked Brutus.

But I was already out the door of Opal's office, and heading down the hallway in the direction of the conference room. I burst in and made a beeline for Odelia.

"It's Kurtz," I told her. "He's the kidnapper. He's the one behind this whole thing!"

Odelia smiled politely at her colleagues as they all turned to her at the sound of my mewling. "I'm sorry. Feline emergency. I think he forgot where his litter box is."

And to laughter from the others, she got up and walked out.

"Kurtz? Are you sure?" she asked the moment we were out of earshot.

"Dooley heard the kidnapper use the phrase 'toodle pip' last night, the same thing Kurtz said when he was at the house a couple of days ago. That can't be a coincidence, Odelia." And then I remembered something else. "At the salon and spa, Prunella said that Kurtz was a regular. And she didn't mean at the salon but at the clinic where they perform plastic surgery. Is it possible that Kurtz used to be a woman and transitioned to a man? And that's why he sounded like a woman when he phoned the salon?"

"I noticed the first day that Kurtz doesn't have an Adam's apple," said Odelia. "You're absolutely right, Max. He's the kidnapper. He's the one behind this whole thing!"

I suddenly heard a noise, and when I looked up I found myself staring straight into Kurtz's eyes. He was standing right behind us! Odelia looked up, and gasped in shock. He then gave her a wan smile, and before she could stop him, was running to the exit!

"Not on my watch!" I shouted, and set off after the guy —or gal.

"Max! What's happening!" shouted Brutus.

"It's Kurtz!" I shouted. "He's the kidnapper!"

To Brutus's credit, he immediately got the message, and alerted the others, who were still inside Opal's office. And then five cats were in hot pursuit, and one reporter, with Kurtz having a head start of mere minutes.

The odds were finally in our favor!

We ran full tilt, but Kurtz knew his way around the studio

lot a lot better than we did, and disappeared into the studio next to Opal's.

As we burst inside, I saw that they were filming some sort of sword-and-sandal action flick, with several men dressed in nothing but leather straps and sandals swinging their swords and trying to hit each other.

Behind us, Odelia rounded the corner, followed at a distance by Gran and… Opal!

"Hank!" I could hear Gran cry, and when I followed her gaze, I saw that one of the men in leather straps was, indeed, Hank!

"Oh, hey, Vesta," said Hank, raising his sword in greeting.

"What the hell are you doing here?!"

"I got a part in *Ben-Hur II*! Isn't it great!"

"You could have called me!"

"Well, I've been so busy auditioning…"

"Cut!" an irate voice yelled. "Cut cut cut! What are these people doing on my set!"

I would have stayed and chatted, but I had a killer to catch!

We raced through the studio, still in hot pursuit, and soon found ourselves on the next soundstage, where none other than Leonardo DiCaprio was standing on the bow of a humongous ship! Across the side of the ship, the words Titanic II had been painted, and in Leo's arms he held a young woman. He yelled, "I'm the king of the world!" and the young babe, whom I thought I recognized as a famous Italian model, giggled excitedly.

"Hey, it's Kate and Leo!" said Harriet, who's a big fan.

"That's not Kate," said Brutus. "That's a younger model."

"I thought Leo died in *Titanic*?" Dooley commented.

"They cloned him!" Prunella said. "See! Cloning humans *is* allowed!"

"Cut! Cut!" a bearded man screamed. "Get those darn cats out of here! Get them out!"

He didn't have to say twice, for we were already out of there, and so was Kurtz.

He'd snuck out the back of the studio building and was now heading for one of those funny golf carts. He hopped on, and was soon zooming away.

"We'll never catch him!" said Dooley.

"Oh, yes, we will!" I said.

Behind us—far behind now—was Odelia, and even further behind was Gran. Of Opal there was no trace. I think she'd dropped out of the race altogether.

We raced after the funny-looking golf cart, with Kurtz looking over his shoulder to see if we weren't gaining on him. When he saw we weren't, he actually stuck out his tongue and yelled, "Catch me if you can, you filthy animals!"

And then, suddenly, a second golf cart came zooming in from the right and slammed straight into Kurtz, sending him flying!

He described a perfect arc through the air and crashed into a wall then crumpled to the ground in a heap.

When I looked up, I saw that the second golf cart was being driven by none other than Opal!

She got out of the golf cart, looking a little shook up herself, her arm still in a sling from the bullet Kurtz had fired at her the night before.

And as she stood over Kurtz, she growled, "Game over, you jerk."

34

"Listen to this," said Opal.

They were back in her office. The police had taken Kurtz away, but before they did, Opal had grabbed his phone. It now lay on her desk. She tapped a button and a familiar voice sounded through her office.

'Delete this message the moment you get it, all right? And aim at the heart. I can't believe she escaped three times already. This time finish the job, or else I'll finish you!'

It was Marilyn's voice!

They all stared at Opal, who looked appropriately grim.

"Marilyn was behind this whole thing?" asked Odelia, shocked to the core.

"It sure appears that way. I already told the police, and they're picking her up as we speak." She shook her head. "Thirty years of friendship and now this. I don't believe it."

Odelia didn't believe it either. Just as she found it very hard to believe Kurtz could have done what he did, but there was no denying it was true. He'd actually confessed.

"He used to be a woman, you know," said Opal now. "His name isn't Jack Kurtzman but Dina Bates. I recognized him the moment he said it. Dina used to work as my accountant. She was bright and smart and I liked her a lot. Loyal. Hard-working. But then I discovered some irregularities. Money missing from my accounts, weird payments, bills for services never supplied. I secretly ordered an audit and discovered Dina had been doctoring the books to the tune of hundreds of thousands of dollars. She spent a couple of years inside and when she got out had a sex-change operation and became Kurtz."

"And applied for a job and was hired," said Odelia.

"Exactly."

"She vowed revenge," Gran said.

"Yeah, which from her perspective is understandable, as she figured I was the reason her career was cut short. I just never thought Marilyn would be involved as well."

"It makes sense," said Odelia. "Marilyn knew every last thing about you. She could have told Kurtz how and when you took your coffee, which car to sabotage, and all about your Botox allergy, which probably isn't the kind of thing you share with your staff."

"No, it isn't, though it's possible Kurtz already knew about that, from the days he still called himself Dina Bates. Office gossip is not to be underestimated."

"Amazing story," said Odelia.

"Are you sure Suzy isn't involved as well?" asked Gran. "She could be the third person in this gang."

"Yes, I'm sure," said Opal. "So, Odelia. Tell me. How did you get onto Kurtz?"

Odelia would have told Opal that it had in fact been Dooley who'd solved the case, but she didn't think that was wise, even with a cat lover like Opal. So instead she said, "Just a hunch. And then when I confronted him, he immediately made a run for it."

"And that sealed the deal," said Opal, nodding. She

slapped the desk. "Well, that's it. I'm going down to the police station to give my statement, and I suggest you come with me."

"What about your show?" asked Gran. "You can't not do your show, Opal. People are depending on you."

Opal smiled. "I think maybe it's time to let go. Let someone else do the show for once. And who knows? Maybe step away from this circus altogether. Get my bearings. I have to tell you that this whole experience has seriously made me question my priorities. Made me think about my life, and the things I still want to accomplish."

"You're not thinking about dropping the show, are you?!" asked Gran, horrified.

"And what if I am? I'm sure there are other things I can do. I've always dreamt of running my own studio, maybe scheduling original content in line with my personal beliefs. I don't have to be a show host all my life, and work for these studio bosses."

"You can be a studio boss yourself," said Odelia.

"Exactly!"

And as they left the building and got into Opal's limo, Odelia had a feeling they wouldn't be back there again. Not any time soon.

The case was closed. Finally!

Opal's driver took them down to the police station—Opal's second limo had already taken the cats home, as there was nothing more for them to do. They could relax now.

At the police station, they were invited to look on as Marilyn Coyn was being interviewed.

Opal clearly found it painful to watch as her friend confessed.

"Yes, I conspired to kill Opal Harvey," said a teary-eyed Marilyn, her hands cuffed.

"But why?" asked a lady detective.

"You know, after thirty years I was sick and tired of playing second fiddle," said Marilyn. "Do you know how it feels to be 'the friend of' all your life? To be known for nothing more than being the friend of superstar Opal Harvey? I frankly couldn't take it anymore. I have ambitions. I want to go places, and I was never going to get there if I kept on living in the shadows of the great Opal. So I decided to do something about it.

"I recognized Kurtz the moment I laid eyes on him. Dina Bates. Obviously he had it in for Opal, and obviously he wanted revenge. So I told him I'd help him get even, if he decided to go all the way and end her. He didn't want to at first. All he wanted was to steal enough money to retire to Mexico or Belize, but I convinced him that stealing Opal's money wasn't enough. She's so damn rich she wouldn't even feel the sting. If he really wanted to get even he needed to finish her off. And so he did. Or at least tried."

"You staged your own kidnapping."

"Yes, I did. Just to make sure no one would ever suspect me. And I told Kurtz that this time he better shoot to kill or else. Of course the idiot missed—and then got himself caught by that stupid Odelia. I should never have told Opal to hire her. I just figured if she was going to hire someone, best to hire a rank amateur. Boy, did I get that wrong."

"But Opal was your friend," said the policewoman. "I mean, how could you?"

Marilyn's expression hardened. "I was never Opal's friend. I was her toy. Her plaything. And so one day I decided that wasn't good enough for me. And that's the day I decided she had to die."

Odelia glanced over, and saw that Opal had already left the room. And maybe it was for the best. To be betrayed by your PA is one thing, but by your best friend of thirty years is quite another.

"What a story," said Gran as they walked out of the police station.

"Yeah, what a story."

"Your editor will be happy. You'll be able to write him up a big juicy scoop."

They'd met up with Opal on the police station steps. "No scoop," said Opal as she pulled her coat tighter around herself. "I know you're a reporter, Odelia, and a damn good one, but I want you to promise me you'll write nothing about this. Not a word."

"But..."

"Not a word," said Opal emphatically. "I don't want my life dragged through the mud."

"I think Marilyn will be more than happy to give interviews from prison," said Gran.

"That's her business. I'll flatly refuse to comment. In fact I never want to talk about this again." And with these words, she walked off in the direction of her waiting limo.

They watched her get in, and Odelia fully expected the limo to drive off. But then the window rolled down and Opal hollered, "Well? Are you coming or not?"

"Phew," said Gran. "For a moment there I thought we were going to have to walk."

And then they got into the limo with Opal and drove off.

35

We were all back in Hampton Cove and happy to be there. Tex was clearly happy, too, for he was flipping burgers as if there was no tomorrow. Half of them were landing in the neighbor's backyard but he didn't seem to mind, and neither did the neighbor's new dog, snapping them out of the air and happily gobbling them down.

"Why is Tex feeding the neighbor's new dog?" asked Dooley.

"I think he's feeling magnanimous," I said.

"I think he has no idea what he's doing," said Harriet with a shake of the head.

She was right. Even though Marge had bought her husband a nice new top-of-the-line grill, Tex was still as hopeless as ever when it came to the art of grilling. His burger patties were either raw or burnt to a crisp. Either way, I liked them. Cats are not as picky as humans. Then again, the Pooles clearly weren't picky, either, as they ate up everything Tex managed to land on their plates. They were probably glad the dog didn't get it all.

"I still can't believe Marilyn would do such a thing," said

Marge, slapping nice big helpings of potato salad on plates and distributing them amongst her family.

"Yeah, that came as a big shock to Opal," said Odelia.

"Imagine having your best friend plot to kill you," said Uncle Alec. "Terrible. More, Marge," he said. "Keep it coming."

Marge darted a hesitant glance in the direction of her husband, but since he was too busy flipping a burger patty, tongue sticking out of his mouth in utter concentration, she did as her brother asked.

It had come to Alec's attention that Tex hadn't been completely honest with him when he fed him the whole 'quadruple bypass surgery' line. His little speech had given the police chief the heebie-jeebies, and the moment he got back to Hampton Cove he'd gone straight to the hospital to talk to a cardiologist and schedule the procedure. Turned out his coronary arteries were just A-okay. Tex had wanted to give Alec a big scare and make him adopt a healthier lifestyle. But of course he'd achieved exactly the opposite.

"So how's the Fitbit?" asked Chase as he clapped his superior officer on the broad back.

"Damn thing broke," Alec grunted.

"How can a Fitbit break?"

"No idea. It was fine one minute and then I got out of the tub and it stopped working."

"Did you check if yours was waterproof?" asked Odelia.

"I guess we'll never know," said Alec with a fine smile.

"You destroyed that thing on purpose!" said Chase.

"No, I didn't. It broke all by itself."

"You don't want to be happy and healthy," said Chase. "That's your problem."

"My problem is that I want to be happy, but all the stuff you keep telling me about being healthy makes me unhappy, so…" He lifted his shoulders in a shrug.

"Do you think Uncle Alec has lost weight?" asked Dooley now.

"I think he gained weight," I said. His trip to LA hadn't done a lot for his diet.

"So what's going to happen to Marilyn and Kurtz now?" asked Brutus.

"Oh, they'll both spend a nice long stretch in jail," I said.

"And good riddance, too," said Harriet.

The whole affair had created a big buzz in the media. Both Opal and Marilyn were very famous people, and the story had resonated with readers and viewers across the world. Opal hadn't returned to her show, opting to step out of the limelight after thirty years of prime-time television, much to Gran's disappointment. She was starting her own network, though, so maybe that was some consolation for her millions of fans.

"I can't believe Dooley solved his first case, though," said Brutus.

"I did, didn't I?" said Dooley, who still seemed surprised.

"Yes, you did," I said, proud of my friend.

"Toodle pip," he said. "It's a nice clue."

"It's an excellent clue," I said.

"It's a super clue," said Harriet. "But even though you're now the big hero, Dooley, you're still going to give me your solo spot, right? You promised?"

"Oh, of course," said Dooley. "You can have my spot, Harriet."

"And mine," I said.

"And you can have mine, too," said Brutus.

Harriet smiled. In fact she looked so happy that I decided right then and there she could sing all of my solos. I mean, I like to sing, but I don't like to sing in front of my feline peers. Harriet likes to shine, and she was shining now, which warmed my heart.

And isn't that what friendship is all about? Giving up a minor pleasure just to see that smile on a friend's face? Or enjoying the fact that your best friend solved a case for once?

I think that's what Marilyn forgot: that friendship isn't about taking. It's about giving. And the more you give, the more you get in return. Isn't that just the strangest thing?

Odelia arrived with more burger patties, straight from her dad's grill.

"These are a little charred on the edges," she said apologetically.

"That's all right," I said. "We don't mind."

"Um… I only have three," she said, frowning. "Odd. I thought I had four."

"You can give mine to Max," said Dooley.

"Yeah, give mine to Max, too," said Harriet.

"And mine," Brutus grumbled, a little more reluctantly.

See what I mean? The more you give, the more you receive. Though in this case I decided to give my portion to the dog next door. Too scorched for my taste.

I know I said cats will eat anything, but there are limits.

And besides. What else are dogs for, right?

EXCERPT FROM PURRFECTLY DOGGED (THE MYSTERIES OF MAX 19)

Chapter One

Victor Ball was wending his way home on his bicycle after an evening spent at his favorite bar. His bike was swaying across the narrow dirt road, as its owner had had a teensy-weensy too much to drink.

Victor, a middle-aged man with a formidable handlebar mustache and a sizable paunch, was singing loudly and out of key. He was in excellent mood, which was not unusual after imbibing his body weight in alcohol, and if he had trouble navigating the road that led to his modest home, where his wife had presumably given up waiting for him and had retired to bed, he didn't show it.

In fact it was a minor miracle that he managed to stay upright at all, but he did, and with every mighty push on his pedals he was another couple of inches closer to home.

And he would probably have made it, without aiming his rusty old bike into a ditch, if not suddenly a dark figure had loomed up large and menacing while crossing his path.

Victor, even though drunk as a skunk, still had the presence of mind to pull his brakes and stare at the figure. It was not the kind of thing a man in his state of inebriation was accustomed to: the figure wasn't merely large and imposing, it was also possessed of the kind of sharp fangs and glittering red eyes one usually only sees in movies. Its furry hide was shiny and thick, its pointy ears erect, its lips drawn back into a menacing snarl.

If someone had asked him at that moment to describe the hideous creature, he would have told them it was a wolf, and a very strange wolf at that, for the creature was walking on its hind legs, its front paws clawing the air with distinct malice in mind.

And then, as the monster threw its head back and howled at the full moon, Victor finally did what any sane man in his position would have done: he uttered a broken cry of anguish and terror, dropped his bike, and ran off in the opposite direction as fast as his weak-kneed legs would carry him.

The monster, meanwhile, instead of pouncing on this easy prey—this plump and juicy victim—continued howling at that big ball of cheese in the sky, then turned on its mighty heel and vanished into the woods, presumably eager to scare another drunkard.

Chapter Two

Marge Poole was cleaning her attic. She'd long wanted to take a broom and a duster to the cluttered space and get rid of some of the stuff that had been piling up there for years, but had never found the time—or the willpower. But when she'd been up there the week before and had almost been crushed by a falling stack of books, she'd decided to tackle the matter head-on. So she'd changed into a set of old clothes, had tied a scarf around her head, and had mounted those stairs with a take-no-prisoners attitude.

And she'd just gone through the first rickety rack, when she'd come upon an old photo album and had been idly leafing through it with a wistful expression on her face.

The pictures in the album were of her and her first boyfriend Jock Farnsworth. She'd known Jock long before she'd ever met her current husband Tex, and seeing those old photos of her and Jock brought back a lot of memories.

And she'd been sitting there reminiscing, having forgotten all about attics that needed to be cleaned out, when a voice suddenly sounded from downstairs.

"Mom! Are you up there? Mom?"

"Up here, honey!" she shouted.

Her daughter Odelia's head came peeping up through the attic door, a quizzical look on her face. "What are you doing?" she asked, glancing around at the cluttered space. "Yikes. Someone needs to clean this mess up."

"Well, I was, actually," said Marge, "but then I came upon this album full of old pictures and I kind of lost track of time."

Odelia joined her and took the album. "Is that you? You look so young!"

"I do, don't I? I was even younger than you are in these pictures. Sixteen, seventeen."

"And who's that guy with you?"

"Jock Farnsworth. We were boyfriend and girlfriend two summers long, until he broke it off and hooked up with Grace Beasley instead." She still felt the sting of betrayal at the memory, even though she'd hardly thought about Jock or Grace for years.

"Jock Farnsworth, as in chicken wing king Jock Farnsworth?"

"Didn't I tell you about him? I thought I did. Or maybe I didn't. Yes, Jock and I were together for a while, until we weren't. But then I met your dad and so all's well that ends well. If I'd stayed with Jock I'd never have met Tex, so it was all for the best—even though I didn't see it that way at the time."

"Imagine that," said Odelia as she leafed through the album. "The richest man in Hampton Cove could have been my dad."

Marge laughed. "Yeah, I guess he could have been."

"Are they still together, Jock and this Grace person?"

"Last time I heard they were."

"I think I've seen his daughter at the office once. She's Dan's goddaughter."

"Oh, that's right. Isn't Jock one of the *Gazette*'s main sponsors?"

"He is. Dan owes a great deal to the Farnsworth chicken wing bling."

"Well, it's all ancient history to me," said Marge, closing the photo album and coughing at the cloud of dust this stirred up. "Want to help me clean up?"

"I can't. I have a meeting with Dan. He told me to come down to the office pronto."

"Did something happen?"

"No idea. Usually when it does he tells me over the phone."

"Better get going then. You know Dan doesn't like to be kept waiting."

"Are you sure you'll be able to handle this, Mom? If you keep going down memory lane, you'll never get this finished."

"Oh, I'll be fine," said Marge. "I'll ask your dad to give me a hand when he gets home."

Odelia descended the creaky stairs and Marge put the photo album in a box with stuff she intended to keep, then took a deep breath and tackled the attic with renewed fervor, this time vowing not to let the ghosts of her dead past snag her attention again.

The Jock episode was ancient history. She'd long ago forgiven him for dumping her for Grace and she now decided not to devote another minute of her time to the man.

"Slow down, Victor," said Chase. "You're not making any sense."

Chief Alec had walked into the interview room and took a seat on the edge of the table. "Still drunk, huh? I thought a night in the drunk tank would have sobered you up."

"I'm not drunk, Chief!" said Victor. "I'm stone-cold sober!" His eyes were wide and red-rimmed, and his large mustache was trembling.

"He's drunk," said Chase. "He just told me the same story he told the desk sergeant last night."

"About the werewolf?" Alec grunted.

"It *was* a werewolf, I swear!" said Victor. "I saw it as clearly as I'm seeing you! He was standing not ten feet away from me, growling and howling and he had these claws, at least three inches long, and his teeth were glittering and dripping with saliva!"

"Yeah, yeah, yeah," said Alec. "I think it's time for you to head on home, buddy."

"But I really saw it! It was going to attack me but I was too quick. I ran and ran and I came straight here—but when I told them what happened they didn't believe me!"

"I know you came straight here, and my desk sergeant put you straight into the lockup, as you were drunk out of your skull, Victor."

"I had a few too many to drink, that's true," Victor

allowed, "but as soon as I saw that monster I sobered up. I swear I'm telling you the truth, Chief. You have to believe me."

Chief Alec exchanged a look of understanding with his deputy, and Chase got up. "Let's get you out of here," he told Victor.

"But... aren't you going to finish taking my statement? People need to be warned. You need to call in the army—the National Guard—the FBI!"

"We'll call in Mulder and Scully," said Chase, as he clasped a heavy hand on the man's shoulder. "And you can tell them all about your encounter with that nasty werewolf."

"And while I talk to this Mully Sculder, you'll hunt that beast down, won't you?"

"Oh, of course we will, Victor," said the Chief with a grin. "We'll go after that thing with everything we've got—don't you worry. This is now my number one priority."

"When the reporters show up, tell them I saw it first, will you? And make sure they spell my name right. That's Victor with a C. And Ball with a B."

"Let's go, Victor with a C," said Chase, and led the man out of the room.

"What a nut," Alec muttered.

Chapter Three

"Just look at it, Max, Just take a good, close look."

I didn't have to take a good, close look. Even from a distance I knew what it was: dog poo.

"It's a disgrace," said Shanille. "An absolute disgrace."

"You're not wrong," I said.

Even though Shanille had come to us with the problem, depositing it in our laps, so to speak, she wasn't the first one to have noticed an issue that was troubling the entire feline community.

Dog poo was a problem that had long irked me, and I'd mentioned it to Odelia many, many times.

"You have to talk to your human," Shanille said now. "She has to write an article about this. These dogs are defacing our beautiful town—they're turning Hampton Cove into the garbage dump of the Hamptons. If this keeps up no tourist will want to visit our beautiful town and then where will we be? In the scrapheap of history! The doldrums!"

"It would be very peaceful," said Dooley, who didn't seem to grasp the big picture.

"I think Shanille is right," said Harriet. "Dog poo is the biggest issue of our time. A major menace to public health and safety. Something we desperately need to address."

"It's pretty nasty," Brutus agreed.

The five of us were standing around what could very well be the largest dog turd I'd ever come across in my long and illustrious career as a cat sleuth. And I didn't even need to take a sniff to know whom it belonged to either: Marge and Tex's neighbors had recently gotten a dog, and I had every reason to believe this turd belonged to that dog.

"People step in it," Shanille pointed out as a man carefully sidestepped the pile of steaming dog dung and shook his head in annoyance. "Cats step in it. We all step in it."

"I don't step in it," I pointed out.

"I step in it," said Dooley.

"We *all* step in it," Shanille insisted.

"Eww," Harriet said as she visibly cringed.

"And then they drag that poo into their homes, and it gets smushed into their carpets and smeared across their nice hardwood floors. It gets dragged into nurseries and kitchens. It ends up in bathrooms and bedrooms. It's hideous, it's gross and it needs to be stopped. I know, for Father Reilly curses about the horrible muck every single day."

"Father Reilly curses?" asked Dooley. "I thought priests weren't supposed to curse?"

"He uses colorful language, but never takes the Lord's name in vain," said Shanille prissily.

Father Reilly is Shanille's human, and runs one of the biggest churches in Hampton Cove. And since many people set foot in that church, I could only imagine the amounts of dog poo they trailed inside.

"Just think about it for a moment," she said now. "Let's take as a very conservative estimate that one out of ten people step in dog poo, and that all of those people drag that poo into my church. That's a lot of dog poo to clean up for poor Father Reilly."

"I'm sure Father Reilly doesn't clean his church himself, though, right?" I said.

"No, he has a cleaning lady, but the principle still stands: someone has to clean up the poo. And why? Simply because dog owners refuse to clean up after their dogs. If you want a dog, you should accept the responsibility and remove the poo," said Shanille with the kind of forcefulness that has served her well as director of cat choir. I mean, if you can wrangle the entire Hampton Cove cat community, you can wrangle anything.

"I don't think it's the owners that should take the responsibility, though," said Harriet, who hates dog poo even more than the rest of us. Her gorgeous white fur is more susceptible to being sullied and soiled than mine or Dooley's or Brutus's.

"You don't?" said Shanille.

"Of course not. Just look at us cats. We do our business nicely and hygienically in a litter box, which is conveniently scented so as not to let the foul stench upset sensitive noses.

Afterward, we clean our tushies all by ourselves. Compare that to dogs. Do they use litter boxes? No, they simply pee against trees and poo on the sidewalk. Yuck! And then, to make matters worse, they don't even clean themselves! Double yuck! So you can see how the responsibility of this dog poo crisis lies with the dogs, not humans."

"I think it might be a shared responsibility," said Brutus.

"No, sweetie pie, if we do our doo next to the litter box, is it Odelia's fault, or Marge or Gran's? No, it's our mistake, and we should be the ones suffering the consequences. But if a dog does his business on the floor, nobody cares! And that's the big issue here."

"So what do you suggest?" asked Shanille.

"I suggest we immediately start a campaign to teach dogs to use a litter box, just like cats. I mean, how hard can it be? If we can do it, dogs can do it, too, right?"

"But dogs aren't as smart as cats," said Dooley. "Are they, Max?"

"No, obviously they're not," I said. "Otherwise they would have learned how to go on the potty a long time ago."

"Human babies learn to go on the potty when they're two or three," said Harriet, "so why can't we teach dogs to do the same? It would save us the agony of having to look at that." She wrinkled her nose as she gestured at the big pile of doo, stinking up the street.

"It's a disgrace," Shanille repeated her earlier estimation. "But I don't know if dogs are even capable of being potty-trained. I mean, like you said, dogs are pretty dumb."

"Yes, but surely they're not as dumb as that," said Harriet.

"This is a historic day," said Shanille, who, as a priest's cat, possesses the gift of the gab. "This is the day when five cats decided not to take it any longer. When five cats took a stand and said, enough is enough! No more! We are going to tackle an issue that has plagued our community for far too long."

Her face had taken on an appropriately earnest expression. "We, ladies and gentlecats, are going to potty-train dogs."

"Yes, we are," said Harriet, sounding cautiously pleased.

"And may the world never be the same again," Shanille added.

"Amen," I said. Shanille always has that effect on me.

Chapter Four

Odelia, after her short detour to her mother's attic, finally arrived at *Gazette* headquarters. She made a beeline for her editor's office and when she burst in, saw that he wasn't alone. A pretty young woman with auburn tresses and refined features sat across from him, looking teary-faced and visibly upset.

"Oh, finally," said the young lady when Odelia entered. "You have to help me, Miss Poole. You have to help me find my mother!"

Odelia blinked. "Um..." She directed a questioning glance at Dan, but the white-bearded editor simply stared back at her, a grim expression on his face.

When he finally spoke, there was a catch in his voice. "I don't believe you've met my goddaughter, Odelia. This is Alicia. Alicia, you know Odelia. My finest reporter."

Odelia would have mentioned she was also Dan's only reporter, but the moment didn't seem to lend itself to levity. Instead, she shook the young woman's hand and took a seat. "Such a strange coincidence. I was just talking about your dad with my mother."

"Marge Poole. She works at the library, doesn't she? She's nice. Very sweet and kind."

"She is," Odelia confirmed.

"Alicia is Jock and Grace Farnsworth's daughter," said Dan. "Her mother has gone missing, and I want you to drop everything and help find her, Odelia. I don't care what you're working on—this is now your number one priority, you understand?"

Odelia didn't understand a thing. "But if your mother has disappeared, shouldn't you go to the police? They're more equipped to deal with missing persons cases than I am."

"I can't go to the police. My father would kill me. He's probably going to be extremely upset that I came here to talk to Uncle Dan, but I simply can't stand it anymore."

"Your father doesn't want to involve the police? But why?"

"He thinks Mama didn't disappear. He thinks she ran away... with her boyfriend."

"Your mother has a boyfriend?"

Alicia nodded. "He's an artist," she said, as if that explained everything.

"And... you don't believe they ran away together?"

"Mama would never leave without telling me. We're very close—we're more best friends than mother and daughter. She wouldn't simply up and leave and not let me know. She simply wouldn't."

She'd pressed a tissue to her nose while tears still rolled across her cheeks.

"Look, it's not because your father doesn't want to involve the police that you can't," said Odelia. "She's your mother, and if you have reason to believe her disappearance is troubling, you should tell my uncle. If you want I'll come with you. Chief Alec is a very nice man and very capable. He'll find your mother."

"My father would never speak to me again. He thinks it's bad enough the servants know, and now to involve the police..." She shook her head. "No way. Besides, what if he's right? What if Mama simply ran away with her lover? The police aren't going to be able to bring her back. She's a grown woman. She'll simply refuse to come with them."

"See what I mean?" said Dan, who was clearly worried about his godchild. "You have to find Grace, Odelia. And if you're worried about expenses, don't be. I'll pay you out of my own pocket to find her."

"And I'll pay you the rest," said Alicia. "I just want to know what happened to her. If she did run away, that's her business. I just want to know, so that I can stop worrying."

"Do you know the name of this artist boyfriend?" asked Odelia, taking out her notebook and pencil.

"His name is Fabio Shakespeare. He's a painter and he lives in a small cottage on our domain. Papa wanted to kick him out when he first started suspecting he was having an affair with Mama, but Mama convinced him not to. My parents have been living separate lives for years. They live in different wings of the house, so it's not as if Mama was really doing anything wrong when she got involved with Fabio."

"What do you know about this Fabio?"

"Oh, he's wonderful. A real genius. You should see his paintings. He painted my portrait, too, and it's the most amazing thing."

She clearly seemed taken with this painter, Odelia thought. "So you didn't mind that your mother was having an affair with him?"

"No, I was happy for her. Very happy. Papa is... a difficult man to live with. Even I find him hard to tolerate. I mean, don't get me wrong, I love my father, but he's very tough and demanding—not sweet and loving, like Fabio, and definitely not a romantic."

Odelia nodded. "Do you think your dad will mind if I ask him a couple of questions and snoop around?"

"No, I think it's fine, as long as you promise not to tell anyone."

"Be discreet," said Dan. "Be very discreet, Odelia. And Alicia, tell your dad I'm not going to print anything about this. This is not newspaper business to me—this is personal."

"Oh, thank you so much, Uncle Dan," said Alicia, as she rounded the desk and gave her godfather a big hug. "I won't forget this."

"It's the least I can do for my precious goddaughter," said Dan warmly.

"So when did your mother disappear, exactly?" asked Odelia.

"Um… the last time I saw her was the day before yesterday. At breakfast. We were supposed to head into town that afternoon to do some shopping, but she never showed up. And then the next day when I checked her room I saw that her bed hadn't been slept in. I decided to tell Papa, who hadn't even noticed Mama had gone missing, and he told me to wait another day, just to be sure. And so this morning, when I told him Mama was still nowhere to be found, he told me in no uncertain terms I shouldn't get the police involved, and that Mama had probably eloped with Fabio."

"Did you check to see if Fabio is gone, too?"

"I did. Immediately. And he's gone. Packed his bags and disappeared."

"So that would suggest your father is right."

"I guess so, but like I said, Mama would never leave without telling me. She simply wouldn't."

"Have you tried calling her?"

"Of course. I've called and texted—but she's not picking up and not responding to my texts. Oh, Miss Poole, you have to find her. I'm so scared something bad has happened."

"I will find her, Alicia," she said, even as she wondered if she was making a promise she wouldn't be able to keep. "Trust me."

ABOUT NIC

Nic Saint is the pen name for writing couple Nick and Nicole Saint. They've penned novels in the romance, cat sleuth, middle grade, suspense, comedy and cozy mystery genres. Nicole has a background in accounting and Nick in political science and before being struck by the writing bug the Saints worked odd jobs around the world (including massage therapist in Mexico, gardener in Italy, restaurant manager in India, and Berlitz teacher in Belgium).

When they're not writing they enjoy Christmas-themed Hallmark movies (whether it's Christmas or not), all manner of pastry, comic books, a daily dose of yoga (to limber up those limbs), and spoiling their big red tomcat Tommy.

www.nicsaint.com

ALSO BY NIC SAINT

The Mysteries of Max

Purrfect Murder

Purrfectly Deadly

Purrfect Revenge

Box Set 1 (Books 1-3)

Purrfect Heat

Purrfect Crime

Purrfect Rivalry

Box Set 2 (Books 4-6)

Purrfect Peril

Purrfect Secret

Purrfect Alibi

Box Set 3 (Books 7-9)

Purrfect Obsession

Purrfect Betrayal

Purrfectly Clueless

Box Set 4 (Books 10-12)

Purrfectly Royal

Purrfect Cut

Purrfect Trap

Purrfectly Hidden

Purrfect Kill

Purrfect Boy Toy

Purrfectly Dogged

Purrfect Santa

Purrfectly Flealess

Nora Steel

Murder Retreat

The Kellys

Murder Motel

Death in Suburbia

Emily Stone

Murder at the Art Class

Washington & Jefferson

First Shot

Alice Whitehouse

Spooky Times

Spooky Trills

Spooky End

Spooky Spells

Ghosts of London

Between a Ghost and a Spooky Place

Public Ghost Number One

Ghost Save the Queen

Box Set 1 (Books 1-3)

A Tale of Two Harrys

Ghost of Girlband Past

Ghostlier Things

Charleneland

Deadly Ride

Final Ride

Neighborhood Witch Committee

Witchy Start

Witchy Worries

Witchy Wishes

Saffron Diffley

Crime and Retribution

Vice and Verdict

Felonies and Penalties (Saffron Diffley Short 1)

The B-Team

Once Upon a Spy

Tate-à-Tate

Enemy of the Tates

Ghosts vs. Spies

The Ghost Who Came in from the Cold

Witchy Fingers

Witchy Trouble

Witchy Hexations

Witchy Possessions

Witchy Riches

Box Set 1 (Books 1-4)

The Mysteries of Bell & Whitehouse

One Spoonful of Trouble

Two Scoops of Murder

Three Shots of Disaster

Box Set 1 (Books 1-3)

A Twist of Wraith

A Touch of Ghost

A Clash of Spooks

Box Set 2 (Books 4-6)

The Stuffing of Nightmares

A Breath of Dead Air

An Act of Hodd

Box Set 3 (Books 7-9)

A Game of Dons

Standalone Novels

When in Bruges

The Whiskered Spy

ThrillFix

Homejacking

The Eighth Billionaire

The Wrong Woman

Printed in Great Britain
by Amazon

82997983R00130